Also Available From Jacy Morris

Fiction:

1000 Pieces of Sweet (Coming Soon)
The Abbey
The Drop
Killing the Cult
The Lady That Stayed
The Pied Piper of Hamelin
The Taxidermied Man
An Unorthodox Cure

One Night Stand at the End of the World Series

One Night Stand at the End of the World
One Night Stand in the Wastes
One Night Stand in Ike

The Enemies of Our Ancestors Series

The Enemies of Our Ancestors
The Cult of the Skull
Broken Spirits

This Rotten World Series

This Rotten World
This Rotten World: Let It Burn
This Rotten World: No More Heroes
This Rotten World: Winter of Blood
This Rotten World: Choking on the Ashes
This Rotten World: Rally and Rot

One Night Stand
at the
End of the World

By Jacy Morris

Table of Contents

A Note About This Series

      One Night Stand at the End of the World did not start out as what you see before you. It was dreamed up during the real apocalypse. Of course, I'm talking about the year 2020, when something materialized out of the ether and began making everyone sick.

      Locked at home with nothing to do other than watch TV and drink beers and be bored, the idea for One Night Stand first entered my head as a screenplay, something that could be done on the cheap showcasing the many talents of my friend Nick Kaiel. Without telling him, I wrote up the screenplay, a less than audacious imagining of this tale before you. It was a simple twenty-page script meant to be filmed in one glorious night, in one take. The comedian enters, does his show, and then goes away.

      Underneath our carport, myself, my wife, and Nick would drink beers, order pizza and goof around with this story, turning and twisting it and finding all the little bits of humor that were hidden away in there. Nick's friend Scott came onto the scene, and offered to help us make it. He was enthusiastic about the idea, as we all were.

      At some point, we got serious about doing it, and in the fall of 2020, with the pandemic still going on, we put the money and the equipment together and made a short film. The entire production seemed cursed from the beginning. On our first day of shooting, we needed a campfire. A drought had pretty much turned the entire state of Oregon into a fire-free zone. But that was ok. We figured we only needed a few minutes, and we had a firepit and a hose. Of course, the lady next door called the fire department on us, but not until we got all the shots we needed. No ticket, no fine. The campfire scene was probably the best footage we got, visually.

From there, we shot some random walking footage for the comedian in random parks and roads throughout Oregon. The weirdness of Oregon is such that three dudes, one of them in a trench coat, with a giant fake sword on his back, can basically walk around anywhere and no one will say a damn thing.

Then came the final shoot, two days at a farm in Newberg, Oregon. The first day was glorious. Nick, being an amazing performer, managed to memorize about 17 pages of stand up, and we recorded the show on Friday night. The next day, despite truly miserable weather, about twenty of my friends showed up all decked out in apocalyptic gear just to help us out. They were our audience. Seeing all these people in their different get-ups lit my brain on fire. The characters I had put on the page became real to me at that point. My friend Hunter's amazing LARPing character of Harvey Barrel became Murdertron. I can no longer imagine what Murdertron was even supposed to be like thanks to his amazing get-up. Look up Harvey Barrel if you want to see what he looks like. My friend Ryan came in a uniquely weird get-up, a fur-lined denim jacket and a gambling visor. Suddenly, Beatums was born. I'm not even sure if Beatums was in the original script or not, or if Ryan just looked so cool that I came up with him on the spot.

Many other cool characters stood out, and through pouring rain, swirling winds, and a muddy set outside, we managed to cobble together the shots where the audience appears and laughs, claps, and in Murdertron's case cries. It was grueling, but still good fun, and when we were finished, Scott edited all the footage into something presentable, and we packed it up to the American Film Market to try and sell it. Unfortunately, the AFM was all digital that year, and it was hard to get the short film in front of anyone who could actually do something with it. I did however sit in a virtual room with a nice Finnish man and discuss his post-apocalyptic western project.

Needless to say, I walked away from the AFM feeling pretty dejected. We had put in a ton of work and asked for a ton of favors to get this thing done, but it didn't seem meant to be.

Rather than quit and waste everyone's work, I decided to take this humble 22-page screenplay and turn it into a book—the book you have in your hands right now. Freed from the constraints of reality, the series grew and the characters evolved. Of course, none of this series would be possible without the help of my friends. So a sincere thank you to everyone involved in One Night Stand: Scott Saunders (for filming and jury-rigging everything), Hunter O'Guinn for lending your character of Harvey Barrel to the Murdertron role, Leif Fuller who is Yokel and one of the nicest men to work with, Keith Hunt for finally managing to sit down straight after the tenth try and for finding the cabin for us to film at, Rin Brock for being a complete stranger willing to come out and have a good time on her birthday!, Matt Brock for accompanying Rin, Ashley and Garrett Anderson (A special shout-out to Garrett for coming up with the name Vinegar Strokes, which is still a nightmare), Jen and Casey Keller (Special thanks to Jen for showing up with a cane after having knee surgery), the Scoles clan, Greg, Wendy, Caleb and Brookelyn, Sasha Cohen for sticking it out, Ryan Gregg for turning a nothing character into the man who would become Beatums Sterling, Donovan Ward, and Stacy Kozaczuk for doing the hair and make-up of twenty people in like three hours. Amazing!

I also want to give a special shout-out to my wife Jen, who is the character of Ajax, and did pretty much everything on set, from providing food, to getting people checked in, to coordinating tents and hair and make-up. I

9

can only imagine what a disaster this thing would have been if you hadn't been there. Another special shout out to Scott Saunders who wore a ton of hats and who had quite a hand in the ideas of the series, including the accidental creation of the name of a certain farmer who has a name like Benedict Arnold, but not quite. Thanks for all the awesome props! And finally, a special thanks to Nick Kaiel for being the comedian. If someone came to me today and said, "I want to turn One Night Stand into a TV show, I would say, "Awesome. But Nick Kaiel has to be the comedian." There is no One Night Stand series without Nick.

Anyway, now that that's all out of the way. I hope you enjoy the stories and the characters in this series as much as I enjoyed writing them! Thank you to all my friends who turned what was on the page into a reality that literally blew my mind. If it's too weird or bizarre for you, you have my friends to blame.

Chapter 1: Another Sunny Day in the Apocalypse

Waking up hurts. It hurts so bad that sometimes I wonder how I can manage to do it every day. Why do I even open my eyes when sleep is so much better than the alternative? These were the thoughts that ran through the comedian's head as he stared up at the shredded roof upholstery of the 60s Chevy Impala he had turned into his makeshift hotel for an evening.

The fabric hung down, exposing the metal struts of the roof. As it dangled in his face, he was tempted to grab the fabric and rip it completely free. *Let the car be stripped down to its bones. Let it be what it really is. Remove the artifice, show what was really underneath there—hard, uncaring metal.* But it had given him a night's shelter, so he left it alone; he was nice like that.

The springs in the bench seat had left his back tight and stiff. Over the course of one restless evening, the tight metal coils had assaulted him with hours of unseen pressure in spots unaccustomed to such wear and tear. With one well-worn boot, he kicked the back door of the vehicle open. It squealed with delight at being used once again. Then he lay there, staring at the roof once more, wheels turning in his mind. Almost apologetically, he snatched the fabric from the ceiling in one quick gesture and shoved it into the pocket of his jacket. Countless pockets dotted his jacket, and in each of those pockets, one could find something interesting, deadly things, hilarious things, practical things. The fabric was none of these, but it was a thing, and in this world that meant it had value. Somewhere, in some shitty shanty town, someone was looking for a piece of fabric right now. Maybe they wanted to make a loincloth for a sex slave, or they wanted to create an eye patch for their mutie kid with the missing eye.

Somewhere, in some dying, inbred town, that piece of useless fabric would be worth something to someone, and that meant it was worth something to him.

Scratching at his unkempt black hair, he sat up. At least, he thought of his hair as black. The last time he had seen himself in a mirror, there had been as much silver as black. Somewhere along the way, his body had begun to age without his permission. With a loud crack, he popped his neck. It popped not because he was getting older, but because sleeping in the backseat of an ancient, rotting car would fuck you all up.

The sun radiated down on the Impala, heating the interior, but not to the point that it was uncomfortable. *Fucking idiot. You slept too late.* He had meant to be on the road at first light when it was safe to travel. Once, he had owned an alarm clock, a magnificent collection of gears and springs he had pulled from a charred home, but he had been forced to give it up after a while. It drew too much attention, and the last thing he needed was to find a horde of the undead standing outside of whatever place he had chosen as a single-serving home.

"You let me sleep too late," he complained.

Look at me. Does it look like I have a fucking watch? a small voice bitched, high-pitched with a hint of teenage-ish insolence.

The comedian regarded the doll head hanging from his jacket pocket with amusement. The doll's face was dirty, smudged with soot from being in the burnt air of the wasteland too long. Everything exposed to the burnt air of the world wound up looking like that now. Its hair was wavy, crimped like the female stars of an 80's music video. The roots of the hair were blonde, the ends a faded pink. Maybe pink was how the doll head had been manufactured… or it might be the faded remnants of someone's blood. The comedian didn't care to unlock that memory.

12

"You think I'm blind? I know you don't have a watch, you don't got any goddamn arms! But surely, even you can see when the sun comes up."

The doll head said nothing, just stared at him with those dead, painted-on, gas fire eyes. She did that sometimes—just ignored whatever he said. Trying to force Oddrey to speak would be fruitless. She only spoke when she wanted to, and if he tried to force her, she would clam up for days, and he would get a migraine that made him want to blow his own brains out. Silence was his enemy. As much as he liked to pretend he was made to be alone, the days where she chose not to speak were the worst ones of his life—well, this life anyway.

He tucked Oddrey into the chest pocket of his jacket and stepped out onto the dry, dusty road. A part of him wondered about the car. Who had driven it out to this nowhere part of the world, and why had they abandoned it? Even before the world turned, this place had been nowhere. He wasn't near any pre-apoc towns. Maybe it had broken down, and the people inside had simply walked off.

The road had long been abandoned. Whatever tire tracks one would expect to see imprinted into its plain, dirt surface had been washed away by weather and time. The car itself had a disturbing collection of mold growing on all the doors' rubber seals. On rusted rims, half-buried in the ground, the earth seemed to be slowly devouring the vehicle.

His boots kicked up dust, and he wondered how much radioactivity might be floating around in those miniscule dust particles. With a finger pressed to the side of his nostril, he blew. Snot shot onto the dusty ground, and he repeated the process for his other nostril, ignoring the sooty globs as they sparkled in the dirt. It was never a good idea to look too closely at one's expectorations, lest one saw blood or flesh. Part of not dying seemed to be preventing yourself from knowing you were dying, deluding yourself into immortality. Once you knew something was amiss, you gave power to that tumor, that wet cough, or that knife-wielding raider. Better to not look too close; ignorance breeds long life.

With delightfully clear nasal passages, he bent down into the car and retrieved a massive sword. Five-feet-long, heavier than cancer and sharp as a razor, his sword was his most prized possession, besides his own wit.

In salute, the comedian lifted the sword up to the sky and watched the hazy, orange sun glint off the steel blade.

"Looks like it's another great day in the apocalypse, Oddrey. I predict a temperature of 80 degrees, a humidity level of 85%, and minimal radiation exposure. All in all, a pretty good day. Not bad for November."

The comedian set the doll head on top of the Impala's rust and white roof, noting for the tenth time that the car still had all its windows. It had been a thousand miles since he had beheld such a sight.

Shaking his head at the new glories of the world, he crowed, "Check this out, Odd."

The comedian stepped into the middle of the road to allow himself room to move. Like a gymnast warming up, he shook out his arms and his shoulders. In a flash, he whirled, the heavy blade of his sword slicing through the air, swinging it from left to right. Soil crunched under his boots as he spun, twisting his wrists to bring the blade up into the air. He brought it down swift and quick, and then he twirled on his heel, delivering a thunderous kick to an imaginary enemy. He moved like this for a while, executing his routine until all his muscles had loosened and he was sure if he needed to kill anything, he would be ready and able.

At the end of his program, he spun the blade by twisting his wrists, ending with a forward chop that would have split the skull of any raider who dared stand against

14

him, whether they were wearing a helmet or not. "You like that shit, Odd? I'm like fucking Conan over here."

He turned to look at Oddrey. She stared at him with those freaky blue eyes.

"Yeah, you liked it."

Whether she did or not, Oddrey wasn't telling.

With a flourish, he finished his routine by pulling a sharp metal object from inside his jacket and flinging it at the trunk of a tree that still clung weakly to life. Its yellow leaves frowned down at the quivering bit of metal, the words "Last Laugh" scrawled poorly in Sharpie on the sides of the ninja star.

"Bullseye," he said to himself as he plopped into the backseat of the vehicle, grunting as the back of his head painfully connected with the roof of the car. Odd tittered quietly at his clumsiness. With a sheen of sweat shining on his face, he reached into the backseat and retrieved his backpack, a dusty black bag with no holes in it. That was the important thing. No holes. A bag with holes was just asking for trouble.

He unzipped the bag and fumbled around inside until he found what he was looking for.

"Let's see what we have for breakfast."

But he already knew. He was just putting on a show for Oddrey. People needed that type of shit in the wasteland. They needed shows and pomp and flourishes and the like.

In his hand, he held a small, plastic baggie filled with broken bits of uncooked pasta. Sure, he could have found some water somewhere, maybe in an overlooked toilet tank, maybe in a stagnant puddle where the radiation was only strong enough to give you indigestion for the rest of your life, but he preferred to eat the pasta this way.

"You know, Oddrey, the key to eating uncooked spaghetti is to take it slow. Let the noodle soften in your mouth."

15

Oddrey said something crass, and the funnyman sputtered, almost spitting his precious pasta into the dirt. When he had recovered, he said, "Don't be gross, Odd. I do the jokes around here. Besides, you oughta be paying attention to what I'm saying instead of thinking up dirty jokes. You don't want to break a tooth out here. A broken tooth can get you killed."

How do you know? Oddrey asked.

"I see it all the time, moron. Raiders with jacked up choppers—they're gonna die by the time they're thirty. Gingivitis, gum infections. That shit gets up in your brain and drives you mad, and that's not even factoring the pain into the equation. Half those raiders are gonna wind up dying like Joey Ramone because they didn't have a fucking toothbrush. You would too if you had teeth."

With his own teeth, he broke off the tip of a piece of pasta and held it between his incisors, letting his saliva soften it up and slowly moistening the noodle with his tongue.

It gave him something to do. It gave him the feeling of an actual repast, a bonafide feast. In the end, he ate the equivalent of one whole spaghetti noodle, and it took him over half-an-hour. Breakfast would be the best part of his day.

When he was done, he held the baggie up to the sun. One noodle left, maybe one-and-a-half. His stomach grumbled at him, and he broke off another inch-long piece of spaghetti and placed it in his mouth. If the stomach complained in the morning, then the stomach got a little extra. Squeaky wheel gets the grease, or the uncooked pasta in this case.

He placed the plastic bag back in his backpack and stood slowly with his hands on his knees to prevent pulling any muscles in his back. It wasn't that he was prone to muscle strains or pulls, or that he had a bad back—he was just careful in everything he did. A pulled muscle could mean life or death.

With his backpack and sword in place, he stalked over to the tree with the yellow-leaves and pulled Last Laugh free after a little wriggling. Later, he would sharpen the blades, but for now, they were still sharp enough to do some damage, and if he wound up flinging Last Laugh, he knew it would be a last-ditch effort anyway.

He set Oddrey in the chest pocket of his jacket, zipping it closed with her hair in the middle so that she could hang from the pocket and view the world around them. Oddrey liked to see the world, what was left of it anyway.

"Come on. Let's see if we can find that town today. Maybe we can get ourselves something better to eat than ancient, dry pasta."

Oddrey said nothing. She knew better than to talk when they were on the move. That didn't stop the comedian from yammering on and on about this and that, trying out new jokes, rehearsing the old.

They trudged through the blighted land, the sun beating down on them in its orange way, burning through the ever-present haze that choked the sky and kept plants in a permanent state of autumn. At the last second, he stepped over a puddle in the road. The water bubbled as if it were cooking on a stove. Mist rose from the roiling water, wafting in his direction. He was careful to avoid the cloud as he didn't know why the turbid water boiled. The sun was hot, but it wasn't that hot. Best to avoid things that didn't make sense, a lesson he had learned long ago… well, he hadn't learned the lesson so much as he had seen someone else learn it with fatal consequences.

The town he searched for was some no-name town to the north. He didn't know how far, didn't know where or when. Time and distance were relative things now. The fabric of the world wore thin. He didn't know what caused it—didn't care one way or another. The only thing he knew was how to deal with it. Knowing the hows or the whys would do nothing for him. Hell, the answers might even break him, you know, if he wasn't already broken.

"Huh?" he asked, stopping in the middle of a stand of blackened, blasted oaks, their trunks leaning north as if they were all attempting to flee from something.

You're broken, Oddrey said.

"I don't feel broken." He patted down his body just to double-check.

Oddrey sighed, and he continued his walk, smiling, the goggles on his face protecting his eyes from the dingy orange rays of the cloud-filtered sun. At least he could protect his eyeballs from the UV rays; no cancer for his eyes, though, he suspected in a year or two, or a decade depending on how the time spun, he would be riddled with tumors from his nuts to his toes. But there was nothing to do about it, so he continued his march.

He crested a rise, stalking over a tangle of desiccated vines that made him nervous. Suddenly, his ankle twisted awkwardly underneath him, and he stumbled. With his arms pinwheeling and a fear of the vines in the back of his head, he managed to maintain his balance. When he looked down to identify the son of a bitch that had tried to kill him—he wouldn't be surprised if it was the vines themselves—he found something ivory and dry gleaming up at him. *A skull. Why is it always a fucking skull?* They littered the wasteland, as common as rocks it seemed. The comedian had seen so many of them they had all begun to look the same, all abnormally small. Part of him thought perhaps some crazy bastard was dogging his steps, planting the same damn skull in his path just so he'd trip over it. He kicked the small skull and sent it toppling end over end. It landed upright, staring at him accusingly.

"I hope you're having fun rotting in hell, you little fucker."

With his hands on his sides and his head thrown back, the comedian laughed, a ridiculous laugh, a movie villain laugh. The show was all for Oddrey. She thought it was funny when he did shit like that.

From somewhere in the dying forest, something emitted a groan. The hair on the back of the comedian's neck stood up; he was familiar with this type of groan. Anyone that was still alive in this world knew what it was—a zombie. Oh, they weren't as deadly as books, movies, and video games made them out to be, but you did not want to get bit by one. Luckily, they had the habit of bellowing like a redneck in a strip club anytime something living came within distance.

The smile faded from his face, his hands dropped from his hips, and he stopped laughing. In complete silence, he leaned his back against a massive cedar tree that stood between him and the direction from where the groan had originated. He drew the mammoth sword free. Side-Splitter he called it. The weapon looked more like an airplane propeller than anything else, not because he wanted to show off or anything, but because that's the way it had to be. It was a functional length. He shook his head to get thoughts of his sword out of his mind. He loved his sword, could spend hours playing with it, but now it was time to do the deed, to use it as it had been intended.

Peeking around the tree trunk, his brown eyes took on a steely glint, and he watched the rotting fucker stumbling through the woods in the distance. Once he had a solid idea of the walking dead's position, he withdrew behind the tree.

"Alright, let's see. One-liners, one-liners." Most people in the comedian's position would see death stalking them, but he saw a chance to practice his craft. He saw a chance to entertain, and even though Oddrey was the only person present, he was determined to put on a show.

As if great one-liners were written in the clouds, he tilted his head back and looked at the sky. His lips moved as he practiced and discarded line after line. Then he smiled. He had it.

"Hasta luego, hombre," he said in a deep, slow voice. Immediately, he shook his head. It was no good. It had sounded fine in his head, but he didn't like the way it played. "Nah, too derivative. That's basically a rip-off of Schwarzenegger in Terminator 2." He hated when this happened to him. The comedian prided himself on not being a hack. Any asshole could just say what someone else had said. Dane Cook, example number one. He needed something better, something more original.

Oddrey spoke then, and his head bobbed in time as he marked her words. He kept a watchful eye on the zombie; it stumbled closer now, and he could make out the details of the fiend. It had once been a man, but now it was a pile of dried flesh shuffling in ripped and useless clothing that only barely hid its ugly bits. White, wispy hair seemed to sprout from its leathery skull, drifting slightly with each shuffling step the zombie took. Like a homing pigeon, it was coming his way, as if it knew exactly where he hid.

Oddrey continued tossing out one-liners. Then she said one that resonated with him. "That's perfect, Odd."

Without hesitation, Odd's suggested one-liner tattooed in his mind, the comedian pushed off the trunk of the cedar. His legs, powered by thick muscles, pumped up and down, sending clouds of dust into the air as he sprinted at the rotting once-a-man. It raised its head, its dead, white eyes fixated on the comedian. At the last second, he shifted to the side, running past the zombie and swiping his Side-Splitter across its neck at the same time. He skidded to a stop just beyond the dead man, dropping to one knee, his sword hanging in the air from his backswing. It hurt to maintain the position like that. The sword weighed a ton when his arms were extended out, you know, because of physics, but it would look cool for Odd. That was important… though he couldn't explain why.

When he heard the man's head fall to the ground, shortly followed by the collapse of its entire body, he stood once again and faced the two-part corpse. Blood dribbled from the blade of his sword and onto the dusty ground.

"Pardon me. My barber skills aren't what they used to be." The comedian's face quirked. He looked confused for a second, and then he spoke, trying to explain the joke to the rotting body in the dust. "You see, because I cut off your head, and maybe I was like… just meaning to give you a haircut… you know, like I was a barber or something."

The explanation felt weak, forced, and he knew he had failed once again. He licked his lips and peered down at the severed head, waiting for it to laugh, to say something, anything, to give him some sign at all that he had scored with the one-liner. But it did nothing but begin the process of decomposition on a molecular level.

His face sagged in disappointment as he craned his neck to look down at Odd hanging from his chest. "That's the last time I let you come up with the one-liner."

He bent down and wiped the blood from his sword using the dead man's shirt, leaving a bright crimson slash across the face of some celebrity or other. He didn't recognize the name of the celebrity or the face. Underneath the disembodied head of the celebrity, the words "For President" were scrawled.

The comedian chuckled slightly. "Couldn't have done worse than the last guy." From the woods, he heard more rustling. It took him a moment to spot the source. No groans came, so he was fairly certain it wasn't one of the dead. Then he spotted it, a root or a vine, something woody snaked his way. The snake-like plant wrapped around a limp arm, dragging the man and his shirt into the thick tangle of vines. Cautiously, the comedian backed away.

"That's our cue, Odd."

He turned and walked through the forest, wary of the broken branches and dried vines on the ground. The comedian would walk all night to escape the forest if he had to. Luckily, it was only a mile or two through the dying autumnal trees, and then he was spit out onto a gravel road. As he stepped from the forest, he thought he heard it sigh with disappointment. He resisted the urge to look back for fear that he would see the trees walking after him, their roots fumbling along like octopus tentacles.

Ahead, he saw the thing he loved best, smoke in the sky. Not the smoke that came from burning radiation craters, but good old-fashioned, human-made smoke. He had found the town.

Chapter 2: Shithole

Yokel loved this patch of grass. It was his very own. No one else in town had the slightest clue of how great this grass was, except for him. They were all too chicken to spend time outside the wall, but not Yokel. Well, it's not that he wasn't chicken; it was more that he had been kicked out. Whenever the sheriff kicked him out of town, he never strayed too far; he just hunkered down in the grass until his supply ran out. It wouldn't do to go off into the woods on his own—he had heard tales of the forest that made his skin crawl.

Though it seemed to weigh a thousand pounds, he lifted his head and squinted to study the woods. "Gives me the goddamn creeps." Yokel drew out the word "goddamn" making it sound more like "god-day-yum." Enjoying the way that sounded in his ears, he repeated the word a few more times, forgetting about the horrors of the forest. Careful not to cut his lip as he had done the last time, he lifted the broken light bulb up to his mouth. It was the only drinking vessel he owned. Inside the light bulb, bright green fluid sloshed around.

He tilted the glass back and let the stinging liquid flow over his teeth. The cocktail stung, but in a good way, a way that made him feel alive. A fuzzy warmth spread through his head, and he settled into himself. When he wasn't on the green, he always felt skittish and nervous, as if something was going to dig right out of the ground and eat him. It had been known to happen before, or so the nomads said when they came to trade their turnips and baubles. When he wasn't three bulbs deep, the world left him quaking in fear. But that wasn't a problem right then. As the liquid wormed its way into his stomach and then into his blood, a gentle peace washed over him pushing all of his fears far away.

Yokel's head bobbed, and his eyelids pulled shut against his will. He collapsed sideways into the cool grass. Somehow, he still managed to hold the broken light bulb upright.

He dreamed of the times before. He dreamed of the movie theater he had worked at, a small theater that only played 35mm prints of cult classic films. Insiders, afficionados, and cinephiles referred to *The Golden Reel* as a repertory theater; everyone else called it a dump. He had loved that job, loved seeing other people who treasured movies as much as he did. Even when only five people showed up for a film like Fulci's *Don't Torture a Duckling*, it was still worth it.

Those people were there because they had an appreciation for the bizarre, the weird. They wanted to see a film the way it was meant to be seen, not on some piddly, 50-inch TV. Like him, those people devoured every frame of a movie, sucking in every aspect of the film from the costumes to the production design. Even if there were only five people in *The Golden Reel*, those five people got more joy watching something like Peter Jackson's *Braindead* than hundreds got at the modern multiplexes watching dreck like Fast and the Furious 1000 or whatever the hell number they had gotten up to. But, alas, his theater was long gone, and thankfully, so was Vin Diesel.

Yokel dreamed of the popcorn in the air popper, dreamed of the melting butter and scooping out bags of fluffy, buttery goodness for the few patrons who came to see something like *Eating Raoul*. He loved to entertain and introduce. He dreamed of standing in front of the crowds, welcoming them to the film as they sat in rickety, piss-reeking theater chairs that were held together with duct tape. His greatest joy in life had been to introduce the films. It made him feel special in some way he couldn't quite explain. But now he wasn't special. He was just another asshole getting fucked up on radiator fluid and wondering how the apocalypse had skipped over his dumb ass.

****

The comedian studied the town for a solid thirty minutes—or maybe it was an hour—or five minutes. He wasn't quite sure. A few years ago, he'd owned a Rolex, taken it right off a raider's cold wrist as the bastard breathed his last breath. For a while, everything had run normally, but then he started to notice something odd about the watch. In an old Baskin Robbins, which at that moment had precisely zero flavors instead of 31, he had stared at the watch as a candle burned. Along the length of the candle, he had stuffed dimes at precise increments to help him keep track of time. What he found had twisted his head a bit. The watch hand sped up and slowed down over the course of an hour, until he finally ripped it off his arm and dashed it against a display case. It finally stopped ticking after the thirtieth swing. In the next town he came to, he traded the watches remains for a dog leash and a set of tweezers, and he was lucky to get that. The going rate for Rollies had declined somewhat since the last of the polar ice had disappeared. It was too shiny anyway, a dead giveaway on the road.

But I'm not on the road now. Gearin' up for town. The town in question was squat, vaguely circular, and fortified as most wasteland settlements were these days. A ribbon of barbed wire ran around the top of its outer wall. No building stood taller than ten feet. That was good for when the wind storms came through, or the sand storms, or the lightning storms—or the blood storms. He had heard about that last in another town. He didn't quite believe it, but maybe it was a thing—maybe.

With the knowledge of someone who knew better than to simply stroll into a settlement, he watched. You had

25

to know what you were getting yourself into, had to know if they were a shoot-on-sight type of place or the type of place that would welcome a stranger with open arms. Despite his profession, the wasteland was still new, or maybe it was old now, and you could never tell how a particular town was going to react to a stranger showing up on their doorstep. It was hard to blame them. The wasteland was rife with stories of settlements brought low by a Trojan raider, a seemingly innocuous stranger who entered some sleepy burgh and in the middle of the night, killed the guards and opened the gate to allow his raider buddies inside.

The performer had seen the aftermath of such a village once. Seen it laid low, bodies lying in the orange sun, rotting for no good damn reason except the people were stupid and trusting. Whenever he was chased away from a city, he didn't take it personally. It was practical and smart; kudos to them. He always felt bad for the people who dwelled in towns that welcomed in strangers with open arms. Sooner or later, they were going to get Trojaned as well.

Outside the wall, on the north side of town, he spotted a pitiful sight, a slight man who had the look of a wastrel about him. The comedian eyed the neon green concoction he drank out of a broken light bulb with disdain. Radiator fluid most likely. Whoever the man was, he wasn't a town guard or anything like that. If he was, his ass would have been fired by now, because soon after his last sip of bright green liquid, he had slumped over on his side and fallen asleep.

On the south side of town, the comedian watched a stooped man hauling a load of lumber on his back walk up to a gate and knock on it. After a brief exchange, someone let the man inside. No one shouted at him or pointed guns at him. These people were playing it pretty loose with security. That meant one of two things. They were either

26

badass and evil, and everyone in the area knew not to fuck with them, or they had a couple of rough and tumble types inside who could take care of business. But that was ok. He could take care of business too if he had to.

You going in or not? Oddrey asked.

"Yeah, yeah." The comedian stood, his knees cracking with age, or maybe some radioactive isotopes had snuck into his knee joints. He wouldn't put it past the sneaky little bastards.

The grass of the wild meadow between the forest and the town rasped against his pants as he strode proud and tall through its stalks. As if he didn't have a concern in the world, he walked straight up to the passed-out wastrel lying in the grass, mostly to show anyone who was watching that he meant no harm.

As he got closer, the unconscious man came into clearer focus. His shirt had once been white, but now it was stained brown, as if it had been soaking in a bowl of diarrhea for some time. Maybe it had. Fresh, functional shirts were rare these days, and beggars couldn't be choosers. On the front of the shirt, he could make out the words *God bless this shithole*.

Gently, he kicked the man in the legs. Well, maybe not all that gently.

The man snapped awake with a start, and he peered up at the comedian with squinted eyes and a furrowed brow.

"I ain't gonna suck it."

"What?" the comedian asked, taken by surprise.

"Oh, uh—nothing." The man's bleary eyes seemed to focus on the comedian for the first time, and he held up a broken light bulb, green liquid sloshing around inside. "You want some Anarchy Juice?"

The comedian eyed the liquid suspiciously; he had no intention of drinking it, but you never knew how important a new person in a new town could be. Even this

27

piece of shit, this wasted, dog of a human might hold some clout in this town. Humoring the man, he asked, "What's in it?"

The man smiled up at him, a touch of pride shading his face. It was a rare sight. "It's a secret recipe. I made it myself."

"Yeah, well, it looks like antifreeze to me."

At this, the man's pride turned to suspicion and annoyance. "Who told you that? Who been tellin' you my recipe?"

The comedian smiled disarmingly, sensing that the man was on the edge of a blowout. "I been to enough towns to recognize a Prestone cocktail."

The man's face shifted from suspicion to amusement and his anger melted away as a smile spread across his face. "This ain't no Prestone! What do I look like to you? Some classless raider with no teeth? This is pure Zerex!" The man cackled and held the light bulb up to the comedian. "Skoll!" He tilted the broken glass to his lips, draining the rest of the green liquid in one go.

With that, the man fell over on his side, apparently forgetting the comedian was even there. Frustrated, the performer smiled a maniac's grin and kicked the man in the legs once more—hard. His eyes glassy and dazed, the man sat up and looked around, somehow surprised to be awake. He finally focused on the comedian just as the comedian kicked him again. A small yelp escaped the man's lips.

"What's the name of this town?" the comedian asked, all pretense of friendliness gone.

The man, now also cranky, waved an arm dismissively in the air. "Cain't you read? It's Shithole."

The comedian looked up, and there, right in front of his face hung a sign crafted with all manner of inconsequential items, from matchbook cars to old combs to spoons and flattened dixie cups. The sign looked like an art project gone wrong. Sure enough, the mismatched

28

collection of items spelled out the word "Shithole," and he realized he had seen the sign before and dismissed it, never thinking that someone would name their town Shithole.

"That's an odd name for a town." But the man offered no response. He curled up in the grass like it was the world's snuggliest pillow, and the comedian shrugged his shoulders. He circled the outside of the town, scoping out the walls. They weren't anything to write home about, bits of plywood bolstered with obsolete metal street signs that served no function. Here there was a deer crossing sign, there a triangular yield sign. A couple of guard towers dotted the circumference, but no one manned them at the moment. He made it to the south gate with no trouble.

With a hand clad in a fingerless leather glove, the comedian knocked on the gate, his fist resounding thunderously off a plywood exterior that felt sturdier than it looked.

"Piss off!" a voice yelled. "You ain't coming back in until you've sobered up. Last time you threw my favorite hat into the fire. You know how rare it is to find a hat that looks just like the one Indiana Jones wore? It's not like there's anyone making hats these days! You see any fucking haberdasheries around here?"

The voice on the other side spoke in a strange southern drawl, and the comedian wondered if the accent were real as he waited for the man to finish his tirade.

"Just give us a knock when you're all straight, and we'll let you right in," the man continued.

Sensing that now was the time to let the owner of the voice know it had the wrong man, the comedian yelled, "Greetings, uhh, whoever you are." The comedian grimaced at his adroitness. "I'm a traveler from down south, and I have some business in your town."

After a slight pause, a small panel in the gate slid open. A pair of red-rimmed eyes peered through the opening in the gate. The eyes were sharp, appraising. "You look like trouble," the man said.

The comedian had dealt with this type before, the gatekeeper, the protector, the person responsible for making sure no less-than-savory types made their way inside the protective walls of the enclave. He understood it completely, and he spread his hands in a disarming gesture, smiled so the man could see all of his perfect white teeth, and ducked a grandiose bow that would have been right at home in the court of Louis the Fourteenth... all that was missing were the high heels and the foot-tall wig.

When the comedian righted himself, he spoke in his performer's voice, a rich, reassuring timbre meant to disarm and feel familiar and friendly at the same time. "I'm no trouble at all, sir. I'm just a humble comedian, traveling the world and bringing cheer wherever I can."

"Yeah, yeah. Last guy that showed up trying to entertain us turned out to be a raider stooge. Opened the gates in the middle of the night—got a bunch of us killed."

The comedian's smile spread wider somehow, and he said, "I can do my show and then leave if you wish."

The guard was unconvinced. "Listen. We ain't got anything for ya. You see the sign?"

The comedian looked up to see another sign of hodge-podge knickknacks and bric-a-brac forming the word *Shithole*. "Lovely name."

"Yeah, well, that ain't no exaggeration. This place is a shithole, and unless you're in the market for shit, you'd best do your act somewhere else."

The comedian allowed the skin of his face to droop dramatically. He rounded his shoulders, slumping down, trying to look as pitiful as he could. "I won't survive another day out here," he pleaded.

"Yeah, well, that sounds like a you problem, not a me problem."

The comedian could read which way the wind was blowing, and he decided to go for broke. "Maybe you know a friend of mine. Cheatums Sterling? He said he was headed this way—

"Aw, boo. Cheatums, he closes the curtains on Sunday."

The comedian's head cocked to the side as he tried to determine exactly what "closing the curtains on Sunday" meant. Nothing came to mind immediately. "What does that—"

"Doesn't matter. Cheatums ain't here," the voice said, clipped and curt. "Just his brother."

Finally, he was getting somewhere. Sensing an in, he pressed forward. "Well, can I talk to his brother?"

"I don't know what Beatums would want with you. He kicks the can 'til it don't come down, if you know what I mean."

"No, what does that mean?"

"You don't know, you won't find out."

The comedian's head was starting to spin. He had no idea what was going on; he just knew he wanted it to stop.

The man moved to slide the board shut, and then, as if a thought had just crossed his mind, he paused, and slid the spyhole open again. "Listen, times is hard all around. I tell ya what. I got somethin' that could maybe use some doin'. You do this thing for me, and maybe I can let you in."

Finally, a ray of hope. The comedian didn't let himself get too high on that ray. He had seen them extinguished in the blink of an eye.

The man plowed on as if he were reading a man his last rites. "Thought that'd get your attention. Listen, it's warm during the day, but at night it still gets kinda cold 'round here. I been fixin' ta make my nuclear chili, only problem is I'm short o' beans. You get me some beans, and maybe I can sneak you in."

The comedian couldn't believe his ears. *Beans? Beans? The musical fruit?* "So, you want me to go on some sort of quest, like this is some sort of video game, get you some beans, so you can make chili and keep warm with—flatulence?"

"Well, don't say it thatta way, kid. You're makin' it sound all sortsa weird."

The comedian shrugged his shoulders.

"Deal?"

The comedian nodded. "Deal."

With that, the man slammed the peephole slat shut.

From the other side of the gate, he called out. "Hurry back, now. You'll wanna get them beans back afore nightfall. Shit gets wild around here when the sun goes down."

****

The comedian stood at the gate for a moment, mulling his options. He could smash down the gate easily. Hell, if he wanted to, he could smash through the very walls themselves. But that wouldn't get him the information he needed, and he was short on food. Sure, he could break down the gate, but he didn't know how many people were on the other side. He was no slouch in the killing department, but a whole town of angry survivors might be too much for him to handle, especially on a near empty stomach.

He shrugged his shoulders. *No reason to kill today, not yet anyway.*

Turning, he walked around the perimeter of Shithole, stopping in front of the passed-out man in the grass. Some of the grass waved and moved on its own, extending and caressing the face of the man on the ground. The sight made the hair on the comedian's neck stand up.

A thin stream of drool ran from the man's mouth, and the blades of grass near his face danced in it, swaying back and forth in the man's green-tinged spittle. The comedian bent down and pulled the man to his feet. With a grunt, he stood the wastrel's limp, skinny body on the heels of his well-worn boots and then slapped him gently on the cheek. He failed to stir, and so the comedian slapped him harder, the sound ringing across the meadow.

"Hey, wake up!" Slap. "Wake the fuck up!" Slap.

The man groaned, his head wobbling from side to side. Finally, his eyes came into focus and he made a move as if to break free from the comedian's grasp, but the funnyman held him tight, knowing that tomorrow, the man would have fingertip bruises on his biceps.

"You know where I can find some beans around here?" he asked.

The man's face screwed up, and it took him a moment to process the question. The comedian resisted the urge to shake him until his eyes rolled out of his head.

"Beans?" the man asked, his speech frustratingly slow.

"Yeah, beans," the comedian said.

The man's eyes finally dilated and focused on the comedian. "What are we talkin'? Navy? Lima? Pinto?"

"Any fuckin' beans'll do."

The man's eyelids fluttered and then slowly drifted closed. The comedian gave him a rough shake to wake him back up. His head rattled off the town's walls and his eyelids opened once more. "Wake up, you narcoleptic fuck. Spill the beans."

At this, the man laughed, a goofy laugh, his lower lip curving up over his upper as he guffawed like a goon. "What are you, a comedian?" the man asked.

The comedian's patience was wearing very thin. Before the end times, he had been known as a patient man, but now things were a little different. When every breath was precious, one couldn't afford to waste time on stupidity. "You don't tell me about the beans, and shit's gonna get real funny, real quick."

The man's eyes curved up and to the right as he tried to access brain cells that probably hadn't been used in quite some time.

"You know… actually I do know where you can find some beans. Back in the day, when I first got here, people didn't like me so much—not like they like me now at least. This was back when people still had supplies. I stashed a few cans o' beans in the trunk of this old white car in case I ever had to run for my life. They're probably still there."

The man's eyes dropped, and he stared at the tips of his shoes self-consciously. "Funny thing though… I can't seem to remember where it was. Too much Apocalypse Juice, I guess."

The comedian let go of the man, and he rocked back on his heels, his legs unprepared to support his entire weight.

He backed away from the swaying man, turned and began to walk away. Over his shoulder he said, "Thanks— what'd you say your name was?"

The junkie called after the comedian as he strode through the grass leading toward the forest. "My name's Yokel! What's yours?"

The comedian didn't bother answering. He was on a quest. He had better things to do, and he fucking hated his name and the past that went with it. He waved at the man. "Keep on truckin'."

Yokel took in the information, processing it in a brain that would look like a moth-eaten piece of cloth if you removed it from his skull and laid it flat. "Keep on truckin'? That's a stupid-ass name." Yokel shambled around to the gate of Shithole. It only took him ten minutes of pleading with the sheriff to get inside.

Chapter 3: A Can of Beans

Eyeing the trees suspiciously, the comedian stepped into the woods.

"Don't eat me, trees. I never did nothing to you." He felt funny saying it—felt like maybe he was losing his mind or had already lost it. But, in the end, he didn't regret speaking the words one bit. If they could eat, they could think, and maybe they knew English, right? They were American trees, had probably been hearing English for hundreds of years. Or maybe they spoke a completely different language, the language of the people that had lived here before Europeans, before Americans. In that case, he had just wasted his breath.

Trying not to notice the subtle movements of branches out of the corner of his eye, he strode through the forest. Retracing his footsteps, he studied the ground for proof of his own passage. If he wanted, he could have relied on his memory to retrace his path. Though he fully trusted his memory, he didn't trust the land, didn't trust that the trees and the roots, or even the rocks, hadn't shifted in the time since he had passed. Having no reason to be sneaky about his arrival, retracing his path was easy enough, even though he was no tracker. To think, there had been food hidden in the car he had slept in. It was better that he hadn't known. If he had discovered the beans earlier, he would have been unable to resist eating them, and then he would have had to search far and wide on some stupid quest for beans.

"Fuckin' beans," he mumbled to himself. "Fuckin' quests. No one can ever just let you into a town. Noooo, they gotta have something first," he lamented.

He stopped in his tracks and peered down at Odd, hanging from his jacket pocket. "Think I'd do that if I ran a town, Odd?"

A grin spread over his face, and he nodded at Odd's whispered idea. "Yeah, riddles. That's what I'd do. Answer three riddles correctly and you get to come into my town. That's how you do it. Monty Python style. Weeds out all the dumb-dumbs too."

Oddrey spoke again, but he was distracted by the sound of shifting leaves. He spun quickly, scanning between the thick trunks of the trees, trying to spot the source of the noise. Whatever it was remained hidden. They were being too clever.

"What was that, Odd?" With his attention split, he paused, listening to Odd while simultaneously trying to hear the sounds of the forest. The woods eerily quiet now.

"I don't know? Why don't zombies eat comedians?"

Because they taste funny.

The comedian let loose a short guffaw. "That's great, Odd. Too rich. You're the best doll head a fella could ever have. You know that?"

Despite the eeriness of the hushed forest around him, he continued stalking through the tree trunks, stepping over the serious-looking vines that snaked across the ground. Vines were bullshit. Never step on a vine. If he ever wrote a wasteland survival guide, that would be chapter one: Vines. A vine can be anything. It could be a trap set by some toothless raider. It could be the living tentacle from a man-eating tree. It could be some mutated snake. No, vines are to be avoided at all costs.

The comedian shook his head and mumbled once more, "Because they taste funny." Giddy, he called out to the trees. "You don't want to eat me. I'm a comedian. I taste funny."

The wind blew, and the trees shook, or maybe the trees shook independently of the wind. It wasn't clear which. The comedian smiled as he strode through the trees. *Yeah, they speak English.*

After sliding down a short rise, he stumbled from the forest onto the gravel road that would lead to the car. Gravel, now there was a thing you could trust, at least he hoped so. In his travels, he had never once encountered anything sinister about gravel, and as an added bonus, it would alert you to anyone following you. Gravel was great.

The comedian broke into a trot, turning on a sustainable burst of speed. Time was important out here. As the sun dipped behind the tree tops, he knew he didn't have much time. The pair of eyes behind the gate had said things got "real weird" at night, as if that particular fact was specific to the land around Shithole. But it wasn't. Nighttime was the wrong time, the bad time, the get dead time.

His lips ached with dehydration, and he hoped they had some good water to buy if he managed to get inside Shithole. But first he had to get the beans.

A strange sound emanated from the woods to either side of the road, and the comedian stopped in his tracks. "What the fuck is that?"

Odd didn't answer.

Hooting—he heard hooting. It sounded like the mating call of some backwoods inbred incapable of forming actual words due to deformities—he had seen a guy like that once, back in Coaltown. But that was a long time ago, and a thousand miles away… maybe farther. He had a feeling the world was growing bigger, spreading. He had seen proof of it before, in the cracks. But he didn't want to think about the cracks. He didn't want to think about anything. He just wanted to grab a can of beans and get back to that shitty little town and inside some walls.

Get your thumb out your ass, Oddrey said.

"You're right. Let's get them beans and get the hell out of here."

The hooting intensified as he picked up his pace. An eerie call and response, the noise drove him to haste.

Peering through the broad tree trunks, he looked for any signs of movement as he sprinted down the gravel road. His eyes registered nothing, but his ears heard a lot of somethings.

In the distance, he spotted the muted shine of a dirt-covered windshield, and he ran as fast he could, no longer concerned about conserving his energy. Speed was important now. Fear bubbled up in his chest, and he hit the side of the white sedan at a full run. He pulled open the driver's side door, wincing as the rusted hinges creaked in the hazy afternoon air.

Despite his panicked state, the smell of the Impala's dusty interior hit him with a wave of nostalgia as he leaned into the car. A memory washed over him, and he recalled a time when he and a crush had snuck into an old abandoned junkyard to fool around among the old relics. With a sigh, he banished the memory. Using his hands as his eyes, he ran his hands along the underside of the dashboard, searching for something that could be the trunk release. All around him, the hooting intensified, raising the hairs on the back of his neck.

Hurry, Odd implored.

Abandoning his quest for a trunk release, he hopped into the back of the car. Sweat poured down his face in the stuffy vehicle as he wrenched on the upper part of the bench seat. The muscles bulged in his arms as unconscious swear words tumbled from his mouth. With a great squeal, the seat popped free, revealing ancient rusty springs. A cloud of dust spread around him, and his allergies kicked in.

There was laughter among the hooting now, and he wondered what fresh hell came his way. He dove into the blackness of the trunk, his hands groping blindly in the darkness. There was nothing there, not even a spare tire or a tire iron. He rested his head against the floor of the trunk, dejection flooding through his body. "Fiddlesticks."

Out of the corner of his eye, he caught a glance of something shiny and metallic hanging from the roof of the trunk. *Duct tape.* With a shaky hand, he reached out and felt something cylindrical under the tape. The shape remained firm when he squeezed it, and his fingertips brushed against the familiar, tell-tale ridges of an aluminum can. Gripping the cylinder, he heaved, and the duct tape came free with a rip. Contorting himself, he backed out of the trunk clutching his found treasure. In his hands, he held not one but two cans of beans. *Success!* He stuffed the cans in his deep pockets where they clanked against all of the other odds and ends he had scrounged for survival.

Shapes moved among the shadows of the forest— too close, and too fast to be the undead. The shades swept through the woods hooting and hollering, and he turned and ran, careless of the noise he made. Stealth wouldn't save him now, only speed.

****

The comedian hit the woods at a full sprint, unconcerned about anything but the noise of his pursuers as they closed in on his position. Behind him, his pursuers crashed through the forest, rustling leaves and snapping old, dead branches. The raiders, their contempt for the world all-consuming, chased him down like a dog, smacking the tree trunks with the flats of their weapons and producing metal clangs that sent chills up his spine. Their hooting surrounded him. In his pocket, he gripped a can of beans so hard, he was surprised it didn't burst open like a can of spinach in an old Popeye cartoon.

Images of grey spinach rainbowing out of a can into Popeye's mouth ran through his head, and then he tripped. His hand flew out of his pocket, and one of the cans of beans went flying as he hit the ground. He scrambled off

40

his stomach and onto his back in time to see a vine coiling around his ankle. *Stupid ass. That's chapter one of the Wasteland Survival Guide you're never going to write.* Kicking to break free, he pulled a knife from his belt. After the first hack at the vine, it uncoiled and withdrew to preserve itself.

The trees trembled around him, raining pine needles and leaves onto the ground. Above, branches shook and vibrated like a simpleton pushed to the point of breaking. The trees of the forest weren't hiding now. Unafraid, they quaked with rage as their branches began to whip through the air. Maybe it was the presence of others in the woods, maybe they were just mad that he had hacked at one of the vines. Maybe the vine was like that shitty little friend every group had, the trouble-maker, small, unbowed, and eternally looking to draw his friends into a scrap. He had taken a swing at it, and now the forest was coming alive to defend their punk ass friend with little man's syndrome.

To his left, a vine scraped across fallen leaves and pine needles, trying to steal his hard-earned beans. "Uh-uh," the comedian said, as he slashed at the creeper with his knife. The blade sliced clear through the vine, and its living end retreated as a scream erupted from somewhere deep in the forest. He reached out and grasped the can, holding it tight to his chest.

Stalking toward the comedian, the first raider appeared, his chest heaving and sweat running down his cheeks to create lines of clean skin in the layer of dirt covering his face. Even though the comedian hadn't even told a joke yet, the man smiled at him, revealing a set of choppers that made the comedian wince. Gripped in the man's hand, he held a wicked chunk of metal, not so much a sword or a knife as it was a ragged bit of wreckage, light and sharp enough to split skin and flesh.

The comedian's eyes slid from the weapon back to the man's smile, and he tried to figure out which was more mangled and twisted. "Missin' a few bars in the grate," the comedian said pointing at the raider's mouth. He couldn't help himself. Jokes just came to him.

The smile transformed into a scowl. It always did when you pointed out a raider's fucked up teeth. *But fuck, if they didn't want to be made fun of, they should probably raid themselves a toothbrush and some fucking toothpaste.* In his anger, the raider chopped at a tree branch, as if that would intimidate the comedian. The scrap metal broke the tree branch in half. Red sap leaked from the tree like blood dripping from a wound, and the branches of the tree sprang to life. In fact, all of the branches of all of the trees came to life.

The tree nearest the raider reached out, and he chopped at the branch, his mouth open and his eyes wide with terror. But the branch was too thick. It curled and flexed in a way that should be impossible for wood, wrapping around the poor bastard's wrist and preventing another swing. Then another branch curled around the hapless man.

At this time, the comedian stood. The forest was alive. All around, the hooting of the raiders had turned to screams. The feet of the man in front of him lifted off the ground, and his arms, now confined by tree limbs, snapped under the crush of the branches. The raider's scrap metal sword fell to the ground. The tree that held the man seemed to flex for a moment, and then a great ripping sound filled the forest. With a thump, the raider's torso fell to the ground, jetting blood from the places where his arms, legs, and head had once been attached.

The comedian saluted the tree, turned, and fled. With a smile plastered to his face, he ran, feeling like a kid playing dodgeball as he dodged tree branches and vines at every turn.

The sounds of pursuit and chopping faded away, and still clutching the can of beans, he stumbled from the forest and into fading sunlight.

Exhausted, he collapsed in the squirmy grass, the blades tickling his forearms. Behind him, the forest had grown quiet, still, and absolutely terrifying. His mind filled with one-liners.

Then Odd said, *Don't.*

Ignoring his own nature and his need for a laugh, he took Oddrey's advice and pushed his body out of the wiggling grass. Without taking his eyes off the forest, he backed away until he had put twenty yards between himself and the trees. Then he turned and ran as the sun went down. He had yet to find a village or settlement that opened their gates after dark, and he didn't expect Shithole to be any different.

In the twilight, he used the can of beans clutched in his hand to bang loud and hard on the gate of the town. Faintly, in the distance, he could hear the hooting of the raiders. They must have turned back, gone the long way around. From the volume of the hoots, they would arrive in a few minutes.

"Who goes there?" the man behind the gate called.

"It's me. I got your beans," the comedian panted.

"Well, why didn't you say so?" The guard's voice felt mocking, and the comedian resisted the urge to drive the can of beans through the gatekeeper's forehead as he opened the gate a crack. The man stuck his arm through the opening in the gate, hand out, palm up.

In his head, he pictured smashing the gate with his shoulder, grasping the man by his wrist, pulling the man to the ground, and then pummeling him with the can until his head was a bloody pulp. But he didn't do that. Instead, the comedian slapped the beans into the man's waiting hand, and the arm withdrew. Immediately the gate slammed shut. From the other side of the gate, he heard the man mutter,

43

"Navy beans? Who ever heard of making chili with navy beans? I know it's the apocalypse and all, but navy bean chili?"

The hooting intensified, and the comedian could see the raiders moving in the distance now. If they got their hands on him, it would not be a good thing. He would bet beans on it.

"So are you gonna let me in or what?"

"Navy beans?" the man whined on the other side of the gate.

The hooting grew louder, and the comedian drew his sword from his back, ready to fight if need be. With his back against the gate, he yelled, "You didn't say what type of beans! You just said beans! Now let me in!" The comedian punctuated the last sentence by banging on the gate with his fist.

"Alright, alright, don't get your fingerless gloves in a bunch." The gate opened and the comedian pushed his way into the town, stooping under a small overhang made from an old, pick-up truck canopy.

He got his first good look at the man. He was small with a scruff of white beard around his jawline. His head was an egg-like oval, and his eyes were beady like a rat's, which matched his snout of a nose. As with most people these days, he was whip skinny. With the gate secure, the man turned and studied him with those beady little eyes. The comedian didn't trust those eyes, not one bit. Both men stood shorter than the average man.

The gatekeeper wore an ill-fitting khaki shirt with a patch on the sleeve that said, "Bend Police Department." He wondered if the shirt had originally belonged to the man, or if he had found it and adopted the persona like Kevin Costner in that one movie.

With the hooting getting louder, the comedian turned around and helped the man slam the gate closed. He leaned against it, panting and trying to catch his breath. He jumped as someone, or something, banged against the wooden gate. The eerie howls scaled in intensity. Where before it had seemed almost playful, it now sounded outraged, hungry, feverish.

"What the hell is out there?" the comedian gasped.

The sheriff, in a patronizingly calm voice, said, "Oh, it could be any of a number of things. Could be a rad monkey from the zoo. Could be sex demons. Not a bad way to go, am I right?" The sheriff elbowed the comedian playfully in the ribs, and the comedian resisted the urge to clock the sheriff in his beak. "But most likely, it's the Flesh Peddlers."

"Flesh Peddlers?" the comedian asked.

"Oh, yeah, you know, it's like every place out there nowadays. We got raiders just like everyone else. Ours call themselves the Flesh Peddlers."

"Why?"

"Don't know. It's not like they sell anyone, so they're not really peddling flesh. Maybe it's Flesh Paddlers? Honestly, I don't know. Never really stopped to ask one of 'em. When they come around, we just sort of shoot arrows at 'em until they go away."

The comedian stood incredulous. "And you sent me out there without any warning."

The sheriff laughed softly, good-naturedly, and said, "Well, you got here without knowin' about 'em. I didn't figure tellin' you would make much of a difference."

Not feeling all that funny at the moment, the comedian reached out and grabbed the sheriff. "I'm gonna break your head open old man, scoop out your brains, and eat 'em with my fingers."

Unperturbed by his threat, the sheriff said, "Now, now. That's against rule number one." With his finger, he pointed at a sign nailed to a spindly tree that shot up out of the middle of town. The hand-painted sign was barely lit by the firelight flickering in an old metal drum.

45

The comedian, distracted by the sign, released the sheriff. His knuckles sighed in relief as he released his grip, and the sheriff stepped back and cleared his throat, straightening his ill-fitting shirt to regain some measure of authority. Red, painted letters stood out on a whitewashed piece of old plywood.

At the top of the sign, the comedian could just make out the words, "The Ten Commandments of Shithole." Below that the sign read:

1. No eatin people, mostly.
2. Murders must be approved by the sheriff.
3. No stealing not even like if you really want it.
4. No cornhole.
5. Don't let the raiders in.

Rules number six through ten simply read, "Reserved."

The sheriff smiled at the comedian, a look of pride creeping across his face. "Rule number four, that one's mine."

"Are you talking about the game or—

The sheriff clapped him on the shoulder. "It's a good rule either way. Multifaceted one might say. Come on, I'll get you set up. We got a room for guests."

With that, the sheriff turned and strode away from the comedian, leading him through town. Shithole was on the smallish side as far as settlements went, but it was larger than it looked from the outside. Everywhere he looked, small trees sprang up from the earth, straight like arrows, their trunks skinny enough for the comedian to wrap his hands around if he wished. Despite that, they looked strong and healthy, as if they alone had figured out the secret to overcoming the apocalypse. Jealousy made his heart beat faster.

The two men wended their way through the small, branchless trunks. The trees shot up into the night sky, their branches only starting some fifteen feet into the air where they fanned out and blocked the green glow of the coming evening, preventing him from seeing the shifting lights of the new aurora, the play of light from radioactive particulates in the stratosphere. Around him, small shacks had been built up against the outer wall. On this side of the wall, he could see that the town's fortifications were stouter than he had first suspected. Iron grates had been affixed to the interiors. These were braced with stout tree trunks buried deep in the earth. Would they stop an armor-clad bus? Probably not, but a bunch of dirty raiders on foot wouldn't have a chance, and he hadn't seen a working vehicle in quite some time, so he let himself relax—slightly.

"Hey, get some arrows into them hooters!" the sheriff called up to a man standing on a platform overlooking the outside of town. He was hidden in the upper branches of the trees, and the comedian felt like a fool for not noticing the man sooner.

"Sure thing, Sheriff Eldoon." The comedian heard the thwack of a bowstring, followed by a pained scream. The sheriff didn't pause and kept moving through town.

Emaciated scarecrows huddled around fires, downtrodden, their faces covered in muck.

All around him, the smell of shit seemed to hang, cloying its way up his nose. A man tending a bubbling still nodded at him, and the comedian nodded back, smiling. It never hurt to put the occupants of a town at ease, and his winning smile went a long way.

Eventually, Sheriff Eldoon came to a stop at a small, uninspiring shack that seemed little bigger than an outhouse. He tapped on the shack's wooden door, his face beaming with pride. "Ah, here we go—the guest quarters."

The comedian felt panic rising inside. "I'm not going in there."

"Well, then you can go out there." The sheriff waved his arm in the air, indicating the great wide wasteland.

Despite his best attempt not to, his shoulders sagged. He couldn't contend with the raiders outside on his own, not in the dark anyway. Fighting his fury, the comedian stepped inside and flung his backpack at the bench, silently hissing inside and hoping he hadn't broken anything. That happened to him sometimes; his anger got the better of him.

The sheriff pretended like he didn't notice the comedian's rage. "I'll come collect you in the morning and show you around. Don't worry, I get up pretty early around here." For a second, the sheriff's face disappeared as he bent to the side and picked something up off the ground outside the shack. The words "Home Depot" were emblazoned on the side of the orange bucket he placed on the wooden floorboards.

Then, in a very serious tone, he said, "If you're gonna go number two, don't just do it on the floor like an animal. Do it in the bucket. We got a pile out back. Helps us keep warm in the winter and keeps the lights running. Kinda where the name Shithole comes from. Nighty night."

The sheriff closed the door, leaving the comedian in relative darkness. Tiny lines of light penetrated the blackness through the gaps in the wooden boards. He was in little more than a six-by-six room. It felt more like a kennel than any place an actual human would want to spend the night.

An odor drifted up from the bucket. Clearly, he wasn't the first person to spend the night in the "guest quarters."

The only other item in the room was a wooden bench that ran along the back wall. It looked about as comfortable as sleeping on a rock, and that's exactly how it felt as the comedian rested his weary bones. The wood creaked under his weight. The entire place was not what he would consider "fine craftsmanship," but it would keep the rain off of him if he needed it to.

He kept his boots, jacket, and pants on, and he laid back, groaning slightly as he felt his spine decompress after another day surviving the wasteland. Through the thin boards of the shack, he heard the faint hooting of the raiders in the distance. It sounded like they were moving away from Shithole, but they would be back—raiders always came back—until there was nothing to come back to.

The comedian despised raiders. It wasn't that they were violent and wanted to kill, rape, or eat everything that moved that bothered him. No, what bothered him was how they went about their business. Raiders were lazy. Rather than grow their own food, they took it. Rather than find their own sexual partners, they stuck themselves in anything that moved. Rather than talk out their problems, they killed. Raiders were worthless, a blight on a blighted world.

The comedian sighed. They were just one problem in a world full of them, and there wasn't anything to be done about them. Trying to find solutions to the world's many problems was an exercise in futility, and he didn't have the energy to waste on errant thoughts.

"Well, we're in," he said.

He pulled Oddrey from his jacket pocket and held her up so a sliver of light splashed across her face and one of her blue eyes.

You sure you want to be in here?

"Don't worry. It won't be like the last time."

That's what you said the last time.

"Well, they started it. I don't care what you say about me, but when you start talking shit about Pauly Shore, then you deserve everything you get."

Who is Pauly Shore again?

49

"We've been over this. Encino Man, Son in Law, Bio-Dome. None of these ring a bell?"

Oh, yeah. Jury Duty was my favorite.

"Jury Duty? That's your favorite? I oughta chuck you in that bucket and dump you in a shit pile."

But then you'd be all alone.

The comedian fell silent for a bit, the word "alone" ricocheting around his skull like a trapped bullet. "Yeah, you're right. Let's get some sleep. Nothin' we can do right now."

I love you.

"I love you too, Odd. Sweet dreams."

The comedian closed his eyes then, sleeping lightly, as he always did.

In the middle of the night, as the sounds outside diminished, and all of the coughing and hacking seemed far, far away, he stood up carefully, so as not to wake Odd. Wincing at every loud groan of the wood beneath his feet, he crept across the floorboards. Slowly, he reached out for the door to push it open. The door refused to open further than a crack, and he heard the plonk of something heavy against the wooden latch. *A padlock.*

He tiptoed back to the bench and laid down, secure in the notion that he could escape the small prison if he needed to. The padlock and the flimsy door wouldn't stop him if he really needed to get out. He pulled his jacket tighter and made sure the handle of Side-Splitter was within easy reach, and then he dreamed of a world that didn't exist anymore, hadn't existed for decades now... maybe longer. Time was like that. Today, he might have walked for a hundred years. In his sleep, he smiled and murmured a single word... "Encino." His voice faded out, replaced by his own soft snoring.

Chapter 4: The Upper Decker

"Wakey, wakey, hands off snakey!" The sheriff's voice, annoyingly cheerful, cut through the comedian's dream with a cliché that had been tired the moment it was first uttered. In his interrupted dream, he had been enjoying a cold beer in a pub with an old friend, so it was easy to understand why he sneered at the older man as he threw open the door to the guest quarters.

Slightly revolted, the comedian couldn't help but notice the disappointed look on the man's face as he glanced at the bucket only to find it empty. Shit was money to these people. He didn't know what they did to make it into fuel, but the fact they could run their generators using their own crap was impressive. Most towns he visited ran on crude oil or solar power, or they went dark at night, burning wood or oil made from animal fat to keep the lights on. Not here. They had genuine electricity, so there must be at least one smart cookie in town.

It wasn't Sheriff Eldoon. That much was for certain.

"So are you gonna tell me where Cheatums went?"

The sheriff looked at him with a pensive look on his face. "Look, I can see you want to get up outta here real quick. Why don't we come to an agreement? You do a task for me, and I'll tell you everything I know about Cheatums. Even introduce you to his brother."

The comedian laughed at the sheriff. "Fuck quests. I'm not gonna be your errand boy anymore. You almost got me killed for a can of beans yesterday, and I don't trust that you'd even open the gate for me a second time."

The sheriff shrugged. "Suit yourself, but you're on your own then. Ain't nothin' for free anymore. Even the air costs to breathe." As if to punctuate this last, he coughed and spit a glob of lung butter into the dirt.

51

With an avaricious eye, the sheriff watched the comedian sort out all of his equipment. When he had his gear situated, the comedian stood and stepped out into the light, lowering his goggles over his eyes to protect himself from the hazy sunshine.

"Have a look around," the sheriff said. "I gotta get to the gate. Don't go causing no ruckus in here. Follow the rules, and you'll be just fine."

"Right, no cornhole."

"Hehe. You got it." With that, the sheriff turned around and stalked off to the gate, walking like a proud peacock. The comedian sneered after him. *Dumbass is gonna get everyone in this town killed one day.* He could have done it last night if he'd wanted to, but he wasn't a raider. He worked for a living.

The suspicious eyes of the townsfolk made his skin crawl as he strolled through the small town. Shithole's inhabitants were scrawny, eking out a meager existence, and they looked at him with resentment, as if he, having seen the world outside, was somehow doing better than they were. How long since any of these people had journeyed outside the iron-plated walls of Shithole? Their faces were downtrodden, sad, and it hurt to see them that way. It was the same everywhere. Even those that survived were dying. How long until humanity evolved into humorless nothings? When that happened, they'd be no better than animals. Laughter made people what they were, and these people needed a good laugh.

The comedian wandered over to a row of picnic tables set up in the corner of the camp. Underneath a blue tarp, a large, dark-skinned lady stood stirring a pot. The aroma of the food hit him hard, and his stomach roiled. He was painfully hungry. In his head, he catalogued all of the bits and bobs he had stashed all over his body. Maybe he could make a trade.

Before he could though, the man from outside appeared, Yokel. His hair stood every which way, and he wondered where the man had slept the night off.

"G'mornin'," the man said.

The comedian sneered at him. He didn't know what Yokel wanted, but knowing that his brain was probably pockmarked and half-eaten by radiator fluid, he doubted the man's words would even make sense.

Turning sideways, he brushed past the man on his way to talk to the cook. Yokel reached out and grabbed his arm, stopping the comedian in his tracks.

In a voice like razorblades slicing through skin, the comedian growled, "No touching," as he resisted the urge to reach for the dagger strapped to his right thigh. He had taken fingers for less… a lot of fingers.

"Oh, I'm sorry," Yokel said as he wiped his grimy hands on his filthy T-shirt, somehow staining the cloth even more. The shirt appeared to be more filth than cloth. If he ever washed the damn thing, it might disappear altogether, leaving behind only a few scraps of thread.

The comedian swallowed his rage and made to continue his walk when Yokel interrupted him again. "Sheriff says you're a comedian."

"Yeah, what of it?"

"Well, I was just wonderin' if maybe you could use some help with your show."

The comedian turned to the scrawny man and stared at him through his goggles. The earnestness on Yokel's face was almost unbearable. "Are you funny?" the comedian growled.

"No… I uhh… well, no, not really."

"Are you clever?" the comedian asked.

"I think you know the answer to that."

"Then what the hell would I want with you?"

"Well, I was thinking you know, you could use like a hypeman. You know, like Public Enemy had Flava Flav."

"I hate Public Enemy."

"Or the Bosstones, you remember them? They had that dancing dude that didn't really do anything."

"I don't need a hype man."

Yokel looked pleadingly at him, and the comedian smelled desperation oozing from the man's sweating skin. The poor bastard sounded like a man begging a 7-11 clerk to use the restroom even though the sign on the door clearly read, *Restroom for customers only.* "Think about it. I mean, it's like advertising. I go into a place, chat them up, talk about how great you are, and then when you get there, you do your show and everyone's so pumped up they shower you with beans."

The comedian was an ass-hair away from seeing how far he could throw Yokel, but then he thought better of it. This was the only chance he'd have to find Cheatums, and he didn't want to mess it up. "You know, maybe you have the right idea. Let's see what you got."

Yokel stepped back, straightened his filthy T-shirt, and then launched into a half-assed spiel. "Ladies and gentlemen, I present to you The Master of Dis-Laughter, the Governor of Guffaws... uh, what's your name?"

"The comedian."

"No, I mean what is your real name?"

"That is my real name. You know any other comedians out there?"

"Well, no."

"So when you say *the comedian*, everyone knows who you're talking about, right?"

Yokel gulped down some of his own green-tinged saliva and then nodded.

"So give it another shot."

"Ladies and gentlemen and those in between, I'm happy to welcome you here tonight for the greatest show since Cop Rock—"

"Uh-uh. Lose the Cop Rock reference. You don't want to get people's hopes up too much."

"Uh, the greatest show since The Big Bang Theory?"

"All the nerds are dead. No one's gonna get it."

"The greatest show since Alf?"

The comedian clapped his hands. "Now you're cookin' with kerosene."

"Are you sure? I mean… like shows with puppets aren't actually well-regarded."

"Just go with it."

"Alright," Yokel said. "Let me start it over."

The comedian could see Yokel's confidence growing. It was a pitiful sight, like watching a shaky-handed drunk finally get his key in the ignition of his car. "Hurry up. I don't got all day."

"Ladies and gentlemen and all those in-between, I'm proud to present to you today, the greatest show since Alf. You've been waitin' for him all day, so without further ado, whatever the hell that is, here he is, the Master of Dis-Laughter, the Governor of Guffaws, the comedian!"

The comedian stood stock-still, staring into Yokel's eyes. He could see the man withering under his goggled glare.

"Well, do I get the job?"

"Work on it. Rome wasn't built in a day."

"Shithole was."

"Yeah, I can tell."

The comedian turned his back on Yokel and approached the lady stirring the pot.

"When will you let me know?" Yokel called.

He ignored Yokel and left him hanging, instead turning his charms to the cook. "Mmmm, mmmmm, what is dat I smell cookin' right dere?"

"Well, it ain't fuckin' gumbo so you can drop that corny cajun accent." The lady spoke with perfect English, and the comedian realized that he had just come off as a fool, maybe even a racist fool. Not a good start. "It's corn-grass soup."

The comedian breathed deep. Then he remembered the grass from outside. "That's not squirmy grass is it?"

The lady turned to him, her hand on her hip, precious drops of soup splattering the dusty ground. "Jackass, do I look like I'd put squirmy grass in my soup?"

"Uhh, no ma'am."

She turned back to the soup, eyeing him periodically as she focused her attention on the pot. "Well, I suppose you'll be wantin' some."

"I would appreciate it."

"It's not free, but you know that. Whatchu got to trade?"

His stomach rumbling, the comedian pulled a small plastic bag from one of the many pockets in his old, military officer's jacket. He had never been in the military, but the jacket looked cool and encouraged people not to fuck with him whenever he went to strange towns. In the plastic bag, a dozen twist ties bounced around. "They're unbent."

The cook held her hand out, and he saw that she had an extra pinky finger growing from the side of her hand. Trying not to be too obvious about avoiding her touch as he dropped the baggie into her hand, he handed her the twist ties.

Squinting at the twist ties, she held the baggie up to her eye, and he recognized the tell-tale signs of retina damage when he saw them. She couldn't see anything outside of a three-foot radius, probably not since the bombs. *Good thing she can cook.*

"This and those goggles you got'll get you all the food I can spare, and one night in the sack with me."

The thought of that mutated digit touching his body made his skin crawl, not literally, though he had seen a guy with that unfortunate condition two towns back, or maybe it was three. "Uhh, the soup is just fine."

A small smirk of dejection crossed her face, but she handled it well. Taking a dirty plastic bottle, she dunked it in the soup with her non-mutant hand, which he was thankful for. "Those twist ties'll get you some broth, but that's about it."

She held the bottle out to him. The green-yellow liquid swirled around in the bottle, and he grabbed it gratefully. "A pleasure doing business," he said.

"If you change your mind about them goggles, you know where to find me."

Smiling big, he nodded and turned around. With his back to the woman, his smile disappeared immediately. Spotting an out of the way spot next to the town's wall, he made his way over and posted up against it, eyeing the town. He tilted the bottle up to his lips, scalding them in the process. Rather than scream and swear like he wanted to, he pulled the bottle from his lips and held it in his hands, bobbing his head coolly just in case anyone was watching him. After that burn, he wasn't going to be able to taste anything for a week. But, on the bright side of things, it wasn't like there was a shitload of stuff for him to taste anyway.

The townspeople strolled by giving him a wide berth. They were the smart ones. They knew better than to get close to a stranger. Sicknesses had been known to rip through settlements like Shithole, gutting them as sure as a nuclear bomb would. All the good medicine, the antibiotics, the aspirin, the codeine, had been used up. It was better to keep your distance these days. For those that weren't smart enough, his pained grimace was enough to keep them away. If you made yourself look like you were in pain, most people stayed away, assuming you had some sort of contagious sickness. In a town like Shithole, they'd probably seen a fair number of their residents shit themselves to death with dysentery.

As he leaned against his post, passing the bottle of piping hot soup from hand to hand, a pair of children emerged from a shack. The smaller one, a girl by the looks of her, pulled a cooler with a plastic school seat riveted to the lid across the muddy turf. A small skull, child-sized, rattled and bobbed on the plastic seat. Behind her, her brother walked, big and lumbering. In his hand, he held a mannequin arm. As they walked by, the boy absentmindedly scratched at his skull with the fingers of the mannequin's hand.

Toys were toys he supposed. He watched them sit in the mud, their eyes locked on the ground in front of them, and a feeling of sadness swept over the comedian. He remembered a time when kids like these would be sitting around, their phones in their hands, texting their friends, playing games, doing anything but looking around the town with those bored looks on their faces. In his mind, he played out their lives, spreading them out like a treasure map on a picnic blanket, knowing the only treasure they would ever find would be death. Children were fine, if you accepted that fact.

He traced the path of the boy's life. It was predictable. The same thing happened to all big children. They grew up big and strong because they were always drafted for menial labor, and then someone would teach them how to fight. Then they became short-lived badasses. If they were unlucky, they would have kids of their own, die, and the cycle would repeat itself with their large offspring.

The little girl's life was less predictable. Men were the worst. If she had a protector like her brother, she might be spared the indignities of the wasteland, might hold onto the one thing she had of value. If her brother was a good brother, he might train her to fight, train her to kill, train her to stab a man in the privates when he wanted his way. If he was smart, he would train her to twist the knife so the man would never get up again.

As he tried to ponder the future of these two children, the boy angled the fingers of the mannequin arm up to his nose and proceeded to try and dislodge whatever booger was causing discomfort in his nasal passages. In his concentration, his jaw sagged open, and two pink tongues fought each other for dominance. He doubted that this particular brother would train his sister appropriately.

Well, that settles that, Oddrey said.

"Maybe," the comedian mumbled. He tilted the still-hot broth up to his mouth and took a sip of the soup. It tasted like a freshly mowed lawn covered in sugar, and while he didn't particularly care for the flavor of it, the hot soup worked its way into his innards, warming him from the inside… that or the water was tainted with radiation and he had just delivered a mega-dose of rads directly to his guts. He'd find out in a day or two if he started shitting his insides out. That's how soup worked these days.

Tilting the bottle back, he drained the last of the broth, and then wandered to a far corner of the town. His eyes were drawn to a makeshift shop set up in a crook of the wall. A man, dressed in an outfit that hurt his eyes, stood behind a table piled high with bits and bobs. The comedian spied a handful of screws and nails, a pair of tweezers, some spent brass, springs, wooden cups and bowls, a few tiny bones, and a set of dice, plastic and numbered.

The dice drew his eyes. The orange sunlight above filtered through the blue-plastic tarp that protected the table from the elements. In the daylight, the plastic shapes glowed like diamonds. He liked them, could have had them if he wanted them, but they served no real purpose, unless they were loaded dice, in which case the only purpose they would serve would be to get him killed eventually. Still, he noted that the man had a complete set, fours, sixes, tens, twenties… but the time for games was over. He was here for information.

"Greetings, wanderer, would you care to peruse my wares?"

The comedian measured the man across from him. He wore a helmet, animated and composed of scrap. He looked like a deranged, robotic puppet made from household items. When he spoke, his mouth moved and lights in the eye sockets of the mask flashed on and off. It was actually an ingenious creation, but it was too flashy for the comedian's taste. Out in the wastes, a man would kill you to own something like that, and the bulk of the costume would slow the shopkeeper down and prevent him from escaping the many terrors of the world.

Ropes of yarn laced with wire hung from the helmet, providing the illusion of hair.

"I'm looking for information."

"Well, you've come to the right place. I have more to sell than just these treasures," he said as he swept his hand over his wares.

"I'm looking for a man named Cheatums," the comedian said. "You know where he is?"

"Maybe."

"Maybes don't make great trades. I'm gonna need a yes or a no."

The shopkeeper nodded and the mouth bits of his helmet flapped, the orange lights in the mask's eyes flicking on and off as he spoke. "Then yes."

The comedian nodded; he had expected no less. Did this man, this shopkeeper, actually know where Cheatums was? Dealing with the merchant was a gamble, but he was a trader, and if there was one thing the comedian knew about traders it was that they never passed up the opportunity to make a trade, especially when it involved information. Giving away knowledge didn't empty out his stall. It was found profit. That didn't mean the shopkeeper knew bupkus about Cheatums, but the man was willing to pretend like he was for a chance at scoring some goods.

"Yes, you know where he is, or yes, you know a guy who might know where he is?"

"Uh, yes?"

The comedian's eyes rolled behind his goggles, and he resisted the urge to rip the helmet from the shopkeeper's head and shove it up his ass. Shopkeepers were universally loathed and loved. If you walked into a town and put the hurt on a shopkeeper, you could expect to find yourself hanging from a tree by nightfall. Shopkeepers were the new priests, the kings of their own personal economies. That this shopkeeper had such a collection of bits and bobs indicated he had been doing this for some time. He was probably an important man in town, maybe the most important.

A flicker of movement in the darkness behind the shopkeeper caught the comedian's eye. He sensed danger there, and imagined a crossbow or some other projectile leveled at him from the darkness. He didn't much feel like dying that day. Though there were plenty of days where he did feel like dying, today wasn't one of them. Instinctively, his hand went into his jacket, his fingertips caressing the smooth steel of Last Laugh.

The shopkeeper's eyes went to the comedian's hand, and the merchant made a subtle calming gesture on the counter with his own hand. Though he couldn't see the guard relax, he knew there was no longer something aimed at him. He didn't know how he knew. Maybe it was a side effect of all the radiated food he had ingested. Maybe he had always had the skill, and it had taken the end of the world for it to become apparent to him.

"I know someone who knows where he is," the shopkeeper said, "but information isn't free."

"Sure it is," the comedian said.

61

"Well, no, not this information."

"Why not this information?"

"Because, uh, because you want it."

The comedian smiled. "I don't really want it."

The shopkeeper gasped in his helmet. "Oh, come on, you were just asking about it a few seconds ago."

"I changed my mind."

"But I have the information you need."

"I mean, you can tell it to me if you want to, but I'm not paying for it."

"Well, give me something. Anything. I have a reputation to keep."

"How about some information in return?"

The shopkeeper scoffed at him. "What information could you have that I'd want?"

"I been around. I know things."

The merchant scanned the comedian up and down, from head to toe. "I don't need sex tips."

The comedian laughed, his voice hitching in his throat, taken aback by the shopkeeper's response. "Not in that get-up, you don't. No, not those type of things. What I mean is that I've been around. I've got information about other places. You're a trader, right? Maybe you want to start trading with other towns."

The shopkeeper rubbed his hands together. "Well, maybe that information is worth something."

"Information isn't worth anything."

"Yes, but aren't we talking about trading information right now? If you're trading something, then it has value."

"No, it's worth nothing. I'm giving you something worth nothing, you give me something worth nothing, and the net value of that transaction is nothing."

The shopkeeper pounded on the table, and the comedian could sense his frustration. "I don't think you know what the word value means."

The comedian leaned in close to the shopkeeper. "I don't think you know that information is an intangible social construct, and as such, it has no worth except that decided upon by the person that holds it."

"Uh, construction? Like a statue?"

The comedian could kill the shopkeeper, could grab him by those stupid rope-hair wires and bash his face upon the counter of his own shop. He could then grip the eye sockets of the helmet and twist quickly and sharply, and the man's neck would break. Then he could pull his helmet off and stomp on his face for an hour... but uh... that's not what he wanted to do. Well, maybe a little bit. "So, you tell me your information, and I'll tell you about the nearest settlement to the south. Maybe you can send your buddy with the crossbow down there."

The shopkeeper glared at him from the depths of his helmet. Then he said, "His brother's in the bar. His name is Beatums, but he's not going to give up his brother. You can count on that."

The comedian stood there, his face blank and impassive.

From the edge of his vision, he saw the shopkeeper's hands tense upon the wooden counter. They stood in silence but for the ever-gust of nuclear wind and the sounds of laughter coming from a dark wooden structure behind him. That would be the bar.

Finally, the shopkeeper had enough. "Well, what about my information?"

"What about it?"

"Well, tell me yours. I showed you mine, you show me yours. Quid pro quo, my friend. Quid pro quo."

"I don't speak Latin."

"It means, uh, I gave you some quid, so now, if you're a pro, and I think you are, you have to maintain the status quo. And the status quo here is tit for tat. Everyone knows tit for tat!"

"It's not like that in other towns."

At the mention of "other towns," the shopkeeper leaned across the counter. "Yeah? What's it like in the south?"

The comedian smiled a wolf's grin at the man and said, "I'll let you know after I get there." With that, he turned smartly on his heel and marched away.

Behind him, he heard the sound of a fist slamming into a wooden table followed by some choice words for the comedian.

The truth was the comedian had been south, but economies were a weird thing. He hated them and liked to upend them whenever he could. There was no reason a shiny, threaded screw should be worth an uncooked package of ramen in one town and worth nothing more than a spoonful of dog slobber in another. The way the comedian saw it, he was doing the world a favor, keeping it realistic, balancing the scales if you will.

A tiny tremor shook the town as he headed to the bar. The spindly trees waved from side to side, and the sign hanging from the bar's eaves wavered back and forth on its chains. The earth did that every now and then. Maybe it had gas from swallowing up all those cities. Eating a meal the size of Texas would do that.

As the comedian approached the bar, he examined the sign still swinging lightly on its chains. A picture of a straining man squatting above a toilet tank annoyed the comedian. "Jesus, does everything have to be shit-related in this town? So hacky." At the top of the wooden shingle, the words *The Upper Decker* had been painted in brown letters. Shaking his head, he stepped under the sign and into the common room of the bar.

The Upper Decker was much like the other bars he had frequented in other towns across the wasteland. Behind the bar, the bartender stood with a gut like a VW bug turned on its side and forearms like Popeye, forged by

64

lifting barrels of malt liquor and grain mash onto the counter behind the bar. The comedian scanned the common room, and his wasteland-trained eyes picked out all of the usual suspects: some fighters, an alcoholic bum, some gamblers, among others. The others were inconsequential, village wasters who would die nameless and unloved.

In the western corner of *The Upper Decker*, he spotted the classic lump of smelly rags splayed on the straw-covered plywood. He couldn't see the man's face, but he knew it was a man. It always was. An alcoholic, down-on-her-luck woman could always find someone to buy them a drink. Men were that stupid. An alcoholic man, on the other hand, relied on the kindness of strangers or the pity of those with hearts. The lump of rags was in hibernation, waiting for someone to wander away from their drink or leave for the night, at which point it would stir on spindly limbs and shamble across the plywood floors to drain whatever nasty concoction was left behind in the bottom of the inn's makeshift mugs.

In the opposite corner of the bar, three large, muscular individuals sat with their heads together, mugs of beers sitting mostly untouched on their table. These were the fighters. The lone male of the trio was big, bald, and looked like he wanted to kick the comedian's face in for no real reason at all. The smaller woman, her face scarred and not at all unpretty, quirked her lip at him, and he felt himself stir down below.

It had been a while… maybe too long. A guy could get a condition if he didn't clean the pipes every now and then. But the outright aggression leveled at him by the third woman put all thoughts of random trysts right out of his mind. This third woman's hair was arranged in a warrior's braid, and she had painted a stripe of red and black across her face so that her jewel-like green eyes seemed to float in the shadows of her cloak's hood.

65

The comedian knew danger when he saw it. Those three were to be avoided at all costs. Even if the cloaked woman hadn't been trying to bore holes through his chest with those eyes, he would have felt the same. Though there was nothing in it, he felt like clearing his throat.

I think she likes you, Odd said.

The comedian didn't respond. Sometimes people reacted funny when he talked to Odd. People were so judgy.

In the middle of the bar, four men lounged around a three-legged poker table propped up with the door from a freezer. They squinted at the cards in their hands with the all the concentration of people with a lot of money on the line. One of those men must be Beatums; he'd bet good money on it—only problem was there was no such thing as good money anymore. For a moment, a flash of the past ran through his mind. He remembered a time when he had sunk all of his money into cryptocurrency, those ethereal bits of monetary magic. When the servers went down in the first disaster, it had all disappeared over night, leaving him mostly penniless.

He shook his head, dispelling the past from his mind. It didn't matter now. One of the men at the poker table cocked an eyebrow at him. He'd been staring at them like a creep. To save face, he flipped the switch, kicking himself into performer mode.

"I'm looking for a man named Cheatums—Cheatums Sterling," he announced in a clear, theatrical voice.

The bartender tossed the comedian a suspicious look. The ends of his fu manchu mustache twitched, and he said, "Cheatums? What the hell do you want with Cheatums?"

The drunken pile of rags in the corner lifted its head for the first time and slurred loudly, "Cheatums doesn't drink from the elbow. He's a shoulder drinkuh." The drunk's voice dripped with maximum derision.

"Aw, boooo! I heard Cheatums wipes from back to front," an old man yelled from the bar, his yellowy mustache fluffy with ale foam.

Another man across the bar raised his glass in salute. "Is that the bad way? I wipe from soid to soid!" he called in a faintly British wasteland accent before bursting into maniacal laughter and tilting his mug to his lips. The mug was actually an ancient two-liter bottle sliced in half, and frothy, piss-colored liquid trickled down the sides of his mouth. That guy was obviously three sheets to the wind already and it wasn't even noon yet.

The comedian didn't blame him. There were no more liquor laws. No one was going to fire you for showing up to work trashed in the morning. Hell, it was the best time to get trashed these days. Much better to stumble around drunk in the daylight than at night when the raiders and the carnivorous puddings came out.

"What do you want with Cheatums?" the bartender asked. "He's a human upper-decker, if you knows what I mean."

For a moment the comedian was taken aback. His mouth fell open as he tried to make sense of all the colorful insults that were being hurled at Cheatums.

From the bar, a tottering old man with the skinniest arms the comedian had ever seen said, "Yeah, Cheatums, he uhh… he put the pants on… uhh, like two legs… you got the pants, and the legs, and there's Cheatums." The old man mimed pulling on pants, and the comedian shook his head.

The homespun colloquialisms whirled around his head until he couldn't make a damn bit of sense out of any of them. Frustrated by their responses, and slightly confused, the comedian lashed out. "Listen, I just need to know if you've seen him! I don't need to know about his pants or his preferred wiping style! None of that!" he screamed. The patrons of the bar looked hurt by the comedian's outburst. The older men at the bar turned their back on him, grumbling. The warriors in the corner went back to whispering with their heads together. The men at the poker table returned to their game of poker, matchsticks and dinner mints piling up on the rickety table. He'd lost them.

"Scream at me—pompous son of a bitch," the man with the foamy mustache mumbled. "I'll scream at you."

The comedian sighed deeply. This was another day in a long line of days that wasn't his. If he measured that line, it seemed it would stretch back to the beginning of time.

"Well, what about Beatums? I heard his brother was here."

At this, the men in the room seem to liven up.

"Yeah, Beatums! He's all wrists!" the bartender yelled, pumping his fist triumphantly in the air.

The old drunk in the back lifted his rags off the bench and added, "That Beatums, tines up with his fork, always."

The comedian's head spun again as the voices piled on, adding their strange homespun accolades in their faintly Michael Caine-ish wasteland accents.

"He always puts carrot in the stew first!"

"Straight shootuh. Drinks from the elbow!"

"Trims the roses from the bottom up!"

Skinny Arms even tried to get into the action. "Yeah, Beatums. He's the reason they invented diesel, because there's like… gas… and petroleum, and boom! Diesel all the way. Vin Diesel!"

The comedian noted there was only one man who didn't join in the praise. He was a skinny man. His chest shook with laughter at all of the sayings. He sported an old denim jacket lined with white sheep's wool around the collar. On his head, he wore one of those casino dealer's hats. Faint daylight filtered through the green, see-through plastic of the visor giving the handsome man's skin a greenish hue. His legs were long, and even sitting down, he could tell the lanky man would tower over the comedian.

His lips quirked in a smile, the tall man gave him the smallest of glances with his eyes, and the comedian instantly knew he was the semi-legendary Beatums.

The hubbub and praise died down, and the comedian didn't fail to note that no one bothered to direct him to Beatums. He still had to figure it out on his own. The comedian grabbed an empty chair and dragged it roughly across the uneven boards. Flipping it around so the back of the chair leaned against the rickety table, he plopped down, cool-kid-style.

The thin man, green light splashing over his angular face, didn't bother to look up at him. Instead, he focused on shuffling a deck of cards, old, frayed, well-used. The comedian wouldn't trust that deck of cards even if it had been brand new. The man's hands move in a torrid flurry of action, his fingers bending, flexing, twisting. The cards danced in his hands, moving so fast the comedian could feel the wind of the man's card wizardry.

"Is your name Beatums?" the comedian asked.

The angular man's hands whirred, the cards whirling in ways the comedian didn't think should be possible. The only sign the man heard him at all came with a sly little wink and a quirk of his lips.

The comedian leaned his ample forearms on the table, keeping a poker face even as the table tilted slightly. "I'm looking for your brother."

Beatums hands whirred faster, and for a second, the comedian thought the gambler had fucked up as the cards flew through the air in an arc. The comedian was no mere novice when it came to sleight of hand and dexterity. He could juggle with the best of them, but Beatums' casual

69

mastery of physics had him on edge. As the cards rainbowed through the air, they landed on the table, one atop another, until the entire deck was sitting as pristine and pretty as a picture on the stained and ripped felt of the poker table.

"Cut," the man said.

Thinking of the sword on his back, the funnyman smiled. *I can cut alright, cut you right in two with all these other drunken louts.* He could feel the eyes of everyone in the bar on his skin. He knew they were all watching. Some of them might even have their fingertips brushing against their weapons, ready to chop him down at a moment's notice. Certainly, the warriors in the corner of the bar had fallen silent.

Thoughts of his sword cleaving the man in two subsided, and he reached out with a steady hand to cut the deck.

The angular man nodded at him, swiped the cards up with a fluid gesture, and then said, "If you want to know where Cheatums is, then you're gonna have to beat me, and no one beats Beatums. Whadya say?"

"I got a feeling playing poker with you is like challenging an eagle to a flying contest." The other men at the table nodded.

"You'd be right there… uhh, I didn't catch your name."

"I didn't catch yours either."

The man's chair scraped against the plywood floor, as he stood up in one smooth motion, doffed his visor, and bowed deep and low. The man had the sort of body that made every movement seem to sing, seem to be part of some dance that no one could ever hope to replicate. "Beatums Sterling, at your service."

"Clearly not. Otherwise, you would have told me where your brother is. What I find amusing is that you haven't even asked why I want to find your brother."

Beatums smiled once again as he took his seat, transforming from courteous gentleman to layabout gambler in the blink of an eye as he spread his long legs under the table. "I don't need to know. Because, once I beat you, you're going to forget about my brother and go on your merry way. Hell, I'll even buy you a drink if you offer a challenge."

The comedian leaned forward, a humorous comeback dancing in his head. "When I'm done with you, they're going to have to change your name to Lose'ums Sterling!"

Beatums head rocked slightly in silent laughter, and around the room, the comedian heard slight sniggering, but this battle wouldn't be fought with words. The gambler knew he would lose at such a game. "So what's it to be then?"

The gambler smiled. "I propose a three-game match, to take the luck factor out of it. Three games of skill. I pick two, and you pick one. Best two out of three gets what they want. You get your information if you win. If I win, you hit the bricks and forget you ever heard the name Cheatums Sterling."

The man held out his hand, and the comedian's lips quirked, fighting back his own rage. The phrase "no handshakes" raced across his brain like an ICBM in the night sky. But these were the rules. This was how the world played. The comedian reached out for Beatums' oddly delicate hand and gripped it. In his mind, he could feel the germs transferring from Beatums' skin to the skin of his palm. But he resisted the urge to pull away. Now was not the time to show weakness.

Weakness could lead to disaster. Both Beatums and the comedian knew they had already started the game. As soon as the comedian had plopped himself down, cool-kid-style in the chair, they entered into a game of dominance and bravado. Confidence was a weapon as much as the

71

sword on one's back. Confidence could cut, each slice wearing an opponent down until they could be finished off easily. He dared not show his fear of germs to Beatums.

Instead, he smiled and said, "What's the first game?"

Chapter 5: The Sword and the Family Jewels

"What the fuck is *Bosses and Offices*?" the comedian asked.

"It's a roleplaying game," Beatums said. "I've been developing it on my own for some time now. I got tired of playing games with monsters and criminals in them. We got enough of those running around here every day. So, I came up with *Bosses and Offices*, a game for those who long for the good old days."

"Oh, come on! I thought we were talking about a real contest, like arm wrestling, boxing, maybe a good, old-fashioned dance off." The comedian was starting to get a bad feeling about this game. He had expected something like a physical challenge, had actually wished for it. He could crush this weakling in an arm-wrestling competition. But *Bosses and Offices*? "How does it work?"

Beatums smiled at the comedian for a second, and for a second, the comedian forgot he was here to beat the pants off the man. The gambler had a thousand-watt smile. "It's a simple game," Beatums said. "All you have to do is make it to the end of the game without getting fired."

The comedian smirked, his chest heaving in silent laughter. "I've never been fired in my life. This is cake."

"You can't quit either."

The comedian had of course stormed out of plenty of jobs in his lifetime. His temper often got the best of him when he had to deal with inferiors, as most bosses were. *Damn. Beatums is good.* "I don't know the meaning of the word quit."

The bartender carrying a tray of green ale chanced by. "Quitting is like when you're doing something, and then it's too hard, and then you stop doing it."

"It's a verb," the skeletal alcoholic mumbled from his dirty robes.

The comedian looked at the two villagers in disbelief. "Yeah, I know what the word quit means. It's an expression. An exaggeration. Hyperbole."

"Ah, ah, ah," Beatums said. "That type of backtalk is likely to get you fired in *Bosses and Offices.*" From his pocket, Beatums produced another deck of cards. He didn't shuffle this with the alacrity that he did the other deck. Instead, he lightly slid the cards across each other, shuffling the way a kid might shuffle. The comedian listened as the cards, hand-made, rasped across each other. Beatums handled them reverently. He got the impression that the deck was the man's most prized possession, although his visor was pretty sweet as well. On the back of the cards, the comedian thought he recognized the pictures from old cereal boxes. As the cards slid across each other, he saw a familiar leprechaun's face smiling at him, the cheery little fuck.

Beatums finished shuffling and placed the cards facedown on the table. This time, the comedian thought he recognized the jaunty blue cap of a certain ship captain on the back of the top card.

"Pick one," the lanky man said, his face as earnest as the comedian had seen it.

"Any one?" the comedian asked.

"Any one. Normally, you'd take the card off the top, but I don't wanna be accused of cheating."

The comedian reached out and smeared the deck of cards, flattening the neat pile and spreading the cards all over the rickety poker table. He derived a certain amount of satisfaction from the quick downturn at the corner of Beatums' mouth.

His hand hovered over the cards, and the comedian couldn't prevent himself from licking his lips in anticipation.

74

"What are these again?" the comedian asked.

"This will be your job card." Beatums produced another deck of cards from the interior of his fur-lined denim jacket. The comedian got the feeling that Beatums' jacket had more pockets than his own even, and that was saying something.

As the comedian contemplated which card to pick, the bartender made his way over. The man's arms were folded across his chest in a way that made it easy to see that he was flexing, trying to look menacing in some fashion. The comedian was not impressed. "Before you get too deep, I need you to buy a drink. No one plays here for free."

The comedian smiled inside. Wasteland bars were the same the world over. Everyone wanted something for nothing. "What about that guy?" the comedian asked, pointing to the alcohol-soaked rags in the corner. "He's not drinking."

The bartender shook with laughter. "His stench keeps the rats out. He serves a purpose. You don't."

The comedian ran his hand through his pockets, peering into the dark recesses of his jacket while preventing the others from looking and spying the objects he had stashed away on his person.

"If you don't have anything, those goggles will do nicely. Should buy you an entire night of drinks."

The wheels turning in his head, the funnyman sat back in his chair. "What about this?" he began. "I give you my goggles as collateral, but at the end of all this, the loser of our little contest has to pay up."

The bartender looked to Beatums for confirmation.

Beatums nodded his head. "It's alright, Mugs. I'm always up for raising the ante, especially when I got a sucker on the line."

The comedian smiled at Beatums confidently. Without taking his eyes off the man, he pulled the goggles from his head and handed them to Mugs. "So what do you got on tap?"

"Squirmgrass Ale," the bartender said.

For the first time, the comedian's confidence was shaken. "Jesus, don't tell me you're making ale from the squirmy grass."

"Well, it ain't squirming after it's boiled. I figure it's safe enough. Besides, the only other crop we have here is shit, and that's not a brown ale I figure anyone wants a part of."

"You're right. Squirmgrass Ale it is!" He tried to sound confident, though the prospect of drinking a beer made from wiggly grass made him somewhat nervous. Everyone else seemed to be drinking it.

"You'll like it," Beatums said with a wink. "Now choose your monotony."

The comedian, his hand still hanging over the cards splayed out on the table, refocused. He tried to feel the cards, tried to use his sixth sense of danger to ignore the ones that might lead him to lose the game. He still had no clue what he was doing, but he would trust his senses, trust his fate to lead him to the right card. When his hand hovered over a card that didn't seem to emit a negative energy, he darted his hand forward and snatched it off the poker table. He drew the cardboard to himself and flipped it around just as Mugs the bartender dropped off the first round of drinks.

Mugs placed the sawed-off two-liter bottles on the table's patched and scratched green felt. Holding his drink up to the light, the comedian examined the swirling, frothy, green liquid through the yellowed plastic.

"Unfiltered?" he asked the bartender.

Mugs smiled, revealing a silver front tooth. "That's the only way. If it ain't hazy, it's lazy."

"It would seem to me that it would actually be the opposite. I mean, you're actually skipping a step."

"Uh, uh… whatever." Mugs picked his tray off the table and hurried to the back of the bar where he set about cleaning out the bottom half of his other "mugs" with a rag that seemed more likely to smear filth around than to do any actual cleaning.

"What'd ya get?" Beatums asked.

The comedian peered down at the card in his hand. On the cardboard, he beheld the worst hand-drawn picture he'd ever seen. It took him a while to make out what he was looking at, and as he tried to puzzle out the picture, he said, "You're lucky you didn't challenge me to an art contest." The drawing was little more than a stick figure sitting behind a shape that vaguely resembled a desk. At the top of the card, two barely legible words were scrawled in ballpoint pen. Along the bottom edge, a series of numbers and letters had been scrawled. "It says, 'Account Manager.'"

"Oooh, tough break, fella." Beatums slammed another shuffled deck down on the table and said, "Pick another card."

"What's wrong with account manager?" the comedian asked.

"You'll see. Pick another card."

Annoyed by being put off, the comedian reached out and smeared the new pile of cards across the poker table. Once again, he relied on his sixth sense to pick another card, though if Beatums was right, it hadn't worked out for him the first time. As he flipped the card around, another rudimentary picture greeted him. This time it was a drawing of a large stick-figure man with a huge gut sneering at him. The name at the top of the card read *Carl Swan*.

"Carl Swan? What the hell is a Carl Swan?"

Beatums smiled at him and said, "Hey, some people are lucky and some people ain't."

From a pocket, Beatums produced a set of twenty-sided dice. They were metallic, solid, and the comedian

77

knew if he used those dice, he wouldn't have a chance in hell of winning. "Hold on. I'll be right back."

The comedian stood up and took a sip from the beer. Despite its seafoam green appearance, it didn't taste all that bad. It wasn't good by a long-shot, and it was somehow warmer than the air in the room itself, but still… he could almost taste the alcohol in it. The hungry eyes of the drunkard across the way lingered on his drink. Locking eyes with the despicable bundle, he hocked a thick loogie into his beer. Would it prevent the drunk from draining his beer while he stepped outside? He doubted it, but at least the comedian would get the satisfaction of knowing the piece of shit had downed his lung butter in the process.

With that done, he left the bar and scurried across the small, wasteland village, shoving a simpleton out of the way. The boy turned and groaned obscenities at him, the two tongues in his mouth stuttering over each other to insult the comedian. The child dropped his mannequin arm and began to cry, but the comedian kept moving. He skidded across the dusty ground and came to a stop in front of the merchant's booth.

The man immediately flicked a switch hidden inside his helmet and the lights in his junk mask came on.

"What do you want?" the merchant asked.

"I came back to apologize." The comedian knew he was in for a certain amount of ass-kissing. Once again, his own surly attitude was coming back to bite him.

"What do you need, waster?" The merchant's words dripped with disdain.

"Nothing. I just felt bad about how we ended things earlier. You gave me information. It's only fair that I give you the information you need."

From under his table, the merchant produced a piece of cardboard and a stub of a golf pencil. The comedian envied them both. "I'm ready," the merchant said.

"About four days walk from here, on the main road, there's a town much like this one."

"What do they make there? What type of shit do they need?"

"It's called Glassgow, with two S's."

"Glassgow, Glassgow, right."

Even if the eyes in the merchant's mask failed to light up, he was sure the glow from the man's actual eyes would have shone from inside the helmet upon hearing the information. "They make glass down there. They walk around wearing glass clothes, glass hats, glass shoes. It's really all they got besides a river that still runs and only dries up two weeks out of a month."

The merchant scribbled furiously as the comedian spoke, the small stub of pencil scratching against the cardboard. The comedian told him everything he knew, the names of the people in town, the layout of the city, the security, the raiders around the town. Wherever there was a village, raiders seemed to gather, as if they inherently knew that somewhere in the world someone was trying to establish order, trying to get back to the way things were. You couldn't have a left without a right—you couldn't have a town without raiders. It's just the way it was.

When the comedian stopped speaking, the merchant stared at his scribblings on the cardboard, and he could sense his excitement. Now was the time to pounce. "I'm ready to make another deal."

The merchant tucked the cardboard under his table, as his masked head cocked to the side. "You know of other towns?"

The comedian nodded. "I do, but they're not worth going to. Nothing to see there but people scratching out meals from dirt and old, irradiated k-rations. No, what I have to offer you is something better."

The comedian left his words hanging. It was a calculated move, the type of move meant to reel the merchant in, sink his cheeks on the hook.

"Well?" the merchant asked, his voice scratchy, almost comical.

"I can give your man directions on how to get to the town without getting killed."

"It's only four days away," the merchant said. "I'm sure my man can figure out how to walk south on a road."

The comedian smiled. He had him. "If your man walks south on that road for longer than a day, he won't have any skin by the fall of the second night. The road is a guide, but only a fool walks on that road. It's a death sentence. Without my directions, he'll never make it."

"What do you want for the information?"

The comedian pointed at the dice on the table.

"You want my jewels?" the merchant asked. "You must be out of your mind."

"They're dice, just plastic dice."

The merchant's head cocked to the side like a confused dog. "They're jewels."

"They're dice!"

"No, they're fucking jewels!"

"Jewels don't have numbers written on the side!"

"Some do, if they're special. And I says these are special."

"Listen, whatever. Just give 'em to me, and I'll give you the details on how to get to Glassgow."

"No dice."

"There are dice, and they're right there, and I want 'em."

"Not gonna happen."

Maybe you can borrow them, Oddrey said.

"Yeah, yeah. That's a good idea."

The merchant cocked his helmeted head as if pondering the comedian's sanity.

Switching tactics, he said, "How about, I give you the information, and then you let me borrow the dice for the evening? When I'm done with them, I'll bring 'em right back."

"Call them jewels," the merchant commanded.

The comedian was halfway to a pithy reply, when Odd said, *Just say it.*

"Right, jewels. Can I borrow your jewels for the evening? In exchange, I'll give you the information so that your man doesn't wind up cocooned in the woods by giant spiders, hobbit style."

As if in deep thought, the merchant scratched at the chin of his mask. "No, I don't think so. These jewels have been in my family decades. You want me to give up my family jewels for some information that may or may not be true. I have no way of verifying that anything you say is fact. No way at all."

"Please let me borrow your family jewels. I'm in a bind here."

The merchant fell quiet, and for a second, the comedian thought that whatever energy source the merchant used to animate his helmet had died. "Leave your sword for collateral."

"You want me to leave my sword in exchange for your family jewels? What good are jewels without a sword?"

"What good is a sword without jewels? Neither of us will be happy until this deal is over."

Muttering under his breath, the comedian unslung his sword, laying it on the table with a thump. It was the longest sword the merchant had ever seen. It was so long there were probably only a handful of men in the world that could wield it efficiently enough to be lethal with it. Oh sure, any jackass could swing their sword around, but to truly devastate someone with your sword, that took years of practice.

81

The merchant slid the dice across the table, but kept his hand firmly on the case. They waited in silence, hoping for the other to relent, the comedian with his hand resting protectively on his sword and the merchant with his hand wrapped around his dice.

They stood that way for some time, and then the comedian told the merchant how to get to Glassgow. He told him about the giant spiders on the west side of the road. He told him about the raider gang that roamed the highway, the Queen Arthurs, an androgynous band of funboys with a penchant for debauchery as well as a taste for human flesh. He told him about the acid puddles and the irradiated ruins where the screams of the dead echoed loudly for anyone that passed by.

When he was done, the merchant removed his hand from the dice, and the comedian snatched them from the table. As he dashed to the bar, the dice rattled in their plastic case. "Family jewels," he muttered under his breath.

Without the sword on his back weighing him down, he was amazed at how fast he moved. Though he moved quicker, he felt naked without it, especially as he pushed through the ratty batwing doors of The Upper Decker.

"Fuck off, you pile of shit!" the comedian yelled as he spied the alcoholic downing the last of his drink.

He leaped into the air and kicked the pile of rags square in his bony, alcoholic chest. The man flew across the room and landed on his back with an "oof." The three warriors in the corner of the bar, their mugs still suspiciously full, stood up, their hands going to their waists. *Maces… very interesting.*

Instead of rushing after the drunkard and beating him to within an inch of his life, as he deserved, the comedian sat down at the poker table—cool-kid style once again.

"Took you long enough." Beatums said. "I tried to tell Rags not to drink your beer, but he's not so good at listening when he gets a whiff of ale in his beak."

"It's no big deal," he said, though inside, he plotted several nasty ways to keep the drunk from ever drinking again.

Behind Beatums, Rags dragged himself to the abandoned corner of the bar. A bit of sour flatulence escaped from his sickly body as he scuttled across the plywood floor like a pregnant cockroach. The trio of warriors, two women and one man, resumed their seats. With their heads together, they took up their conspiratorial whispering once more. He'd have to keep an eye on them. They seemed to be up to something, and he suspected they were talking about him in those hushed tones.

The comedian opened the plastic case and pulled out two twenty-sided dice. In a flash, Beatums snatched his own dice off the table, and they disappeared inside his coat before the comedian could even think to watch where he put the metallic icosahedrons.

"Mugs! Another round!" the comedian called.

Beatums smiled at him. "Another round indeed… of *Bosses and Offices*!"

With that, all of the patrons of the bar turned their heads in their direction, and the game was truly begun.

Chapter 6: Bosses and Offices

So, in this game, you're the employee and I'm the head of Human Resources.

-Sounds thrilling.

Don't be so glib. Once we get started, something like that can get you fired. Your goal is to make it through the day without getting axed—

-That's not too different from a regular day. Plenty of raiders with axes out there.

Pay attention. You have stats on your character card. You're an account manager named Vern Wanger.

-Wanger? Seriously?

I don't make up the names. They just come to me.

-So you do make them up.

Now listen. It's the middle of the morning, a Tuesday morning, the most dreaded day of the week. Right now, you're lying in a bed. It's a platform bed, plush and soft, maybe too soft. You got it at IKEA, twenty-percent off.

-That's a hell of deal.

It would be if it was a good bed, but it's an IKEA bed, so your back is sore and knotted, and instead of a good night of sleep, you've had an entire evening of tossing and turning. Your boss, Carl Swan, has been riding you hard all week. The Clive account is due today, and though you tried to go to sleep early so you could get up at the crack of dawn, you didn't fall asleep until one in the morning. It's six now. Your alarm clock goes off, that cruel harpy of sleep deprivation. It bleats like a robot with its dick caught in an electrical socket.

-Robots don't have dicks.

Well, if they did, that's what your alarm would sound like. You have a will stat of ten. If you roll a ten or higher, you wake up on time. Roll.

7

84

Your alarm bleats and bleats, but your body, wracked with stress and needing more sleep, rolls over of its own volition and smacks the snooze button. It looks like you're going to be late for work.

-Oh, come on. Anyone who's worth a shit has two alarms, sometimes three. You don't get to be as successful as Vern Wanger, Account Manager, if you don't have a little foresight.

Funny you should mention that. You have a foresight stat of 12. Roll to see if you remembered to set your other alarms.

    12

-It's a tie, what does that mean?

Your secondary alarm on your phone goes off fifteen minutes later along with the alarm on your nightstand. You roll over and turn the alarms off. With a yawn, you get up. You look over and see your wife lying on your bed. She's not wearing a top.

-How did you know I had a wife?

I didn't. We're talking about Vern Wanger here.

-Fuck you. Who told you about my wife?

We're just playing a game here. This is just Bosses and Offices, man. Calm down.

-Don't you tell me to calm down! I'll calm you down! Talking about my wife. You piece of shit. I tell you what. I'll roll for it. What's Vern Wanger's attack stat? A 5? Good. I'll roll this motherfucker, and if I get a five or higher, I'm going to smash your spying face in!

Whoa, whoa, whoa! This is just a friendly game. There's no reason to get all bent out of shape.

    4

-You're so lucky.

You uhh, you skip out of the bedroom, shower, shave, and then grab a cup of coffee in your favorite mug.

-Oh, man. Coffee. I'd kill someone for a mug of coffee.

You grab your keys from the table next to the door, and with coffee in hand, you get into your car.

-What type of car is it?

You sure you're not going to freak out if I tell you?

-Psshh, what are you talking about? Freak out? I was just playing. I mean you're still lucky I rolled a four.

You drive a Dodge Charger. It's a few years old but you haven't had any problems with it. Your work is about fifteen miles away. You have a menial labor stat of 3.

-Why's it so low?

Low is good in Bosses and Offices. Easier to make your dice checks that way. Vern Wanger is a master of menial labor. He's lived his entire life doing odd jobs and making a very meager living from his diligence.

-Nice.

Roll to see if you make it into work without incident.
20

Whoa! Critical roll! Excellent! The road seems to open up for you. Every light is green, and cars seem to get out of your way as you drive to work. Despite the fact that you woke up fifteen minutes late, you make such good time that you roll into the parking lot right on time. With a little luck, your boss, Carl Swan, won't even notice you as you enter the door.

-Fuck Carl Swan.

You're lucky no one is around to bear witness to your malediction, though many of your co-workers share the sentiment. Carl Swan is surrounded by sycophants who slurp his bottom whenever they get the chance. His network of "Yes-Men" is large and devoted. As you exit your Dodge Charger, you see one of these "Yes-Men," Dave Bigelow, exiting his own car. He is big and round, he waves hello at you with a shit-eating grin on his face.

-Uh… good morning, Dave.

Dave waves back. It's always good to get on the right side of the "Yes-Men," and today seems like a nice day to kiss a little ass. You say...

-You ready for another Tuesday?

It's time for a Kiss-Ass check. You have a Kiss-Ass stat of 11.

9

-Shit.

Dave Bigelow looks at you, his round belly seeming to quake with anger. "You know how I feel about Tuesdays, Vern? It's the worst fucking day of the week. The weekend is so far away, I'm still hung over from my Monday night reality check, and you know it's the day when Carl Swan reviews the numbers."

-Sorry about that. I forgot.

Bigelow peers down his crooked nose at you, a sneer spreading across his ruddy, alcohol-bloom cheeks. He says, "Well, you better not forget about the Clive account. If you don't get that shit on Swan's desk by 5 P.M., your ass is grass." With that, Dave Bigelow takes a sip from his coffee and waddles into the office. You follow, eager to get to work.

Inside the office, it is cool, almost too cool. Carl Swan is known for liking to keep the office running at a chilly 68 degrees. He thinks it makes people more productive, as they tend to work harder to heat up. Your numb fingers know that Carl Swan is wrong, but he's the boss. You say hello to your co-worker Nancy as you sit down at your desk. Nancy's wearing a short skirt, if you tilted your head just right maybe you could see something.

-Forget it. I got work to do.

Nancy, feeling ignored, comes to stand next to your desk. From the corner of your eye, you spot a delicious thigh peeking out from under her skirt. Her shirt fairly bursts at the buttons. "Hi, Vern," she says flirtatiously.

Even though Nancy knows you've been married for years, she still flirts with you nonstop.

-What is this Penthouse letters? This scenario is clichéd and sexist.

Uhh… no it's not.

-Are you playing out your twisted male fantasies on me?

It's just a game.

-That's the problem with guys like you. You do whatever you want, and it's all fun and games until you get called out.

Do you want to win or not?

-I don't want to; I'm going to.

Then play the fucking game.

-Fine. Fine. But I got your number, swine.

Nancy isn't going away any time soon.

-I say… uhh… "Hi, Nancy. I've got to get this Clive account finished, no time for chit-chat."

"Chit-chat?" she asks, somewhat put out. "I just came by to let you know that Carl Swan was looking for you. He seemed pissed."

-Fu… I mean, I better go and see what Swan wants.

You stand from your desk. Nancy leans in close, making it almost impossible to get past her. You notice not for the first time that she has a wonderful smile.

-I say, "Excuse me," and turn sideways to slide past her.

Do you go crotch or butt?

-Seriously?

Seriously.

-Crotch. Always crotch.

Who's the pig now?

-Yeah, yeah.

Vern Wanger, not the most dexterous person, attempts to brush past Nancy, the office flirt. Roll for dexterity. You have to beat a 15.

88

-Get a fifteen or beat a 15?
You need a sixteen or above.
-Damn.
15
You brush past Nancy, lightly brushing your crotch against her backside. She presses against you, and you turn and run from your cubicle in a panic. You look over your shoulder once to see Nancy smiling at you. Your day has just begun.

****

Carl Swan's office is a shrine to white male culture. He's watched Wall Street at least a hundred times and fancies himself the Gordon Gecko of New Bedford Insurance. His office is ostentatious and filled with things that let you know just how manly he is, from his bowling trophies to the stuffed largemouth bass hung way too high. His desk alone would cost you a month's salary.

The man behind that desk is a ball-busting bastard who only seems happy when he's breaking someone down. He has close-curling dark hair, bags under his eyes, jowls like a bloodhound, and constantly reeks of old cigar smoke and coffee. Sometimes you think the only reason he hired you was because he hates you and enjoys treating you like shit. You stand in his office, thinking of a way to introduce yourself.

-You wanted to see me, sir?

Carl Swan looks up at you from his massive marble desk. He sneers at you, and his thick lips quiver with rage before he says, "I did want to see you, fifteen minutes ago, but you weren't at your desk. Right now, I don't want to see you, but here you are. What's the news on that Clive account?"

-I'll have it on your desk by five, sir.

Carl Swan licks his thick lips once before saying, "You better. Or it's your ass." You turn and scurry away from the office with your tail tucked between your legs. Your co-workers look at you with a combination of sympathy for your plight and relief that they're not you.

You return to your desk and prepare for a long day's work.

****

...you've prepped the file, the numbers look good. Now it's time to get this sucker printed out and copied for Carl Swan and the other managers. You pick up the stack of papers from your printer and head over to the copy machine. As you're heading there, a man in a smart looking suit, thin as a whip with a balding head and a pencil-thin mustache heads in your direction. His eyes lock onto you despite your best intention to not be seen. "Vern! Just the man I was looking for. Can you step into my office for a second? I need to talk to you about something." You follow the man to his office. On a cheap plaque, velcroed to the door, you read "Mark Lofton, Human Resources."

Lofton invites you to take a seat. Still clutching the Clive account in your hands, you lower yourself into the world's most uncomfortable office chair, wondering what the hell is going on. Lofton takes a deep breath and smiles at you apologetically. He begins. "Vern, I received a complaint about you from Nancy earlier today." Lofton falls silent as you become more and more uncomfortable. "Nancy says that you brushed against her with your crotch."

-Uhh… uhh… I was just trying to get past her. She was in the way. It was an accident.

Lofton looks at you with a small amount of compassion. It's the smallest amount of compassion that one could muster and still call it compassion, but at least

90

it's something. You're going to have to come up with something better than that.

-I would like to file a counter-complaint about Nancy. She's been harassing me for years.

"Do you have proof of this?" Lofton asks.

-Yeah, last year, Nancy, at the office Christmas party, Nancy gave me a card with a dirty picture of herself in it. She's been trying to get in my pants since she got here.

Do you still have this card?" Lofton asks. Roll for foresight. You need a 12 or above to pass.

14

-Fuck yeah.

Luckily, for you, you foresaw a day when your constant rejections would lead Nancy to try something like this. You walk to your desk with a withering glare for Nancy. She glares right back at you, licking her lips in a suggestive manner. You walk to your desk and fumble around in the drawers until you find Nancy's dirty Christmas card. You return triumphantly to Lofton's office and plop the card on the desk. He picks it up, and stares at the picture for a long time, an uncomfortably long time. Then he says, "I'll talk to Nancy. You're off the hook for now."

You pick up the Clive account and head off to make copies. It's 4:45. You only have fifteen minutes to get the account to Carl Swan.

****

...You successfully swap out the empty toner cartridge, press the copy button on the copier, and watch the second hand spin around the clock, inching its way toward your doom. The whir of the machinery, the click of the copier, the smell of freshly copied papers, and the heat from the copier all make your head swim. Just when you think you're not going to make it, the machine finishes the

91

job. You pick up the copies of the file and hastily move to place them all in a plain white binder. Roll for menial labor.

   4

  Oooh, that was close. You snap the metal binder rings closed, pinching your finger, and then you hustle off to Carl Swan's office, the seconds ticking faster and faster. You push into the office, the binder in your hands.

  Carl Swan spins around in his luxurious, Corinthian leather office chair. In his hand, he holds a picture of your wife. "I walked by your desk today and spotted this little gem sitting on your desk. She's a looker, Vern. What say you and your wife come over to my house for dinner this evening. Maybe we do a little swapsies, if you know what I mean."

  -Don't talk about my wife.

  Carl Swan sneers at you. "Who the hell are you to tell me what I can and can't talk about? If I wanna talk about your wife, I'll talk about her. If I wanna talk about her breasts, I'll talk about them. If I wanna talk about her mouth, I'll talk about it. I'm motherfucking Carl Swan, son of Don Swan and the biggest piece of meat in the office if you get my drift!"

  -I said don't talk about my wife!

  What's she like down there, Vern? Tell me. I want a preview of what I'm in store for.

  -You're gonna die, Swan. I attack Carl Swan.

  20

  Ooh, critical hit. You smash Carl Swan in the face with the Clive account. He totters in place blood gushing from his nose. He is a mountain of a man, swaying like a tree. He crashes backwards, the bridge of his nose jammed into his brain. From behind, Swan's personal assistant spies you standing over the dead Carl Swan. At least he's not talking about your wife anymore. You pick up the picture, knowing your time at New Bedford Insurance is

over. You are most definitely fired, and the only way you'll
see your wife again is through a set of iron bars.
    -Shit.

Chapter 7: Blackout Drunk

With a crooked, knowing smile, Beatums Sterling said, "Oooh. Tough break. You were so close. You just had to turn in the report."

The comedian, panting, his brain awash with rage, finally realized he had lost the game, that he had let his rage get the better of him once again.

Odd, never one to pass an opportunity to point out the comedian's flaws said, *Nice going, dipshit.*

"You cheated. Are you sure you're not Cheatums?"

"I may be a lot of things, my friend, but a cheat is not one of them. You lost fair and square. You had me sweating there for a second."

The comedian, his head awash with a cavalcade of random thoughts looked down at the table to find he had put away a good half-dozen pints of Squirmgrass Ale. Before the end of the world, before the animated teddy bears with razor-sharp teeth, he could have put away a river of the stuff and still driven home. But now, his head was spinning, and he realized the tactical error he had made. He had drunk too much. With the world twisting about him, he stood.

At that moment in time, it seemed as if the entire world were out to get him, and he just wanted to flee, sleep it off, and come back the next day.

"Alright, you ready for round two?" Beatums asked.

"Turmurrow," the comedian slurred as he staggered to his feet. He swiped the dice off the rickety poker table and into his hand, then stumbled from the bar, smashing through the batwing doors with more force than was necessary. The wooden batwings smacked off the clapboard walls of *The Upper Decker*, and he realized he had been playing for longer than he thought. It was dark outside, the stars obscured by the green-glow of radiation clouds.

The comedian stumbled to the merchant's stall. The window was closed and the goods were all locked away safe and sound in the merchant's metal shanty. He pounded on the tin walls. From inside, he heard a clatter, accompanied by a light round of swearing. Then the window to the merchant's stall snapped open. The merchant stood there, staring at him from his mask. "What is it?" the merchant snapped.

"Jesus, you sleep in that thing? I've… I've. I got yer dice here, and I wanted to be giving of them back to you." This last was accompanied by a small, comical hiccup that seemed to shake the comedian's entire body.

"My god, you're wasted."

As the comedian set the dice on the table, a sharp whistle cut through the night air. The merchant stopped talking and listened, the mouth of his mask hanging open and his eyes wide with fear. Another whistle shot through the darkness, followed by another and another. The comedian, even in his inebriated state recognized the whistles for what they were.

"Shit, raider attack." The merchant snatched up the dice, slammed the stall window closed, and from inside, the comedian heard the scrape of metal on metal as the man secured his abode with a padlock.

"Hey! What 'bout my sword, you sumbitch?" The comedian staggered in front of the merchant's store, as the world tilted left and right. "Fucking thief! I'll mooder you!" He tried to figure out if it was the ground actually tilting or if he was just drunk. The extra brainpower required for such a deliberation pushed him over the edge, and he found himself doubled over, retching violently. Green foam sprayed from his mouth as his stomach collapsed in upon itself. He gripped his knees with his fingerless gloves to keep himself from falling into his own mess.

Now you did it, moron, Odd said.

"Did what?"

The hooting around the town grew louder, and now it was accompanied by violent banging against Shithole's protective walls.

From outside, he heard a voice, deep, violent, in command. "Little turds, little turds, let me in! Or I'll huff and I'll puff and I'll blow your door in!" The last word was accompanied by an embarrassing amount of forced laughter. Even in the apocalypse, there were Yes-men everywhere.

As his head throbbed and the world attempted to right itself, the comedian groaned. "Abso-tivo-tutely revolting. Furry tale references furm a raider. So clurver. What's next? a Jeff Furxworthy-inspired, 'you might be a raider' routine?"

The door to the merchant's store popped open, and out came the merchant in full regalia. His outfit, a mishmash of items that made him look like a junkyard version of Optimus Prime, clanked and clinked as he ran through the town. From inside the shadow of the doorway, the comedian spied the pointed tip of a crossbow bolt aimed squarely at his face.

He waved weakly at the shadowed individual inside, and then turned around. He heard the door close softly behind him. The sound of deadbolts driving home was not soft at all.

In the distance, he spotted Sheriff Eldoon climbing one of the small guard towers. Iron plates hung from the rickety edifice, and the sheriff was decked out in medieval-looking armor fashioned with all the craftsmanship of a kindergartner's macaroni necklace. He brandished a rusted revolver in one hand, but he doubted the sheriff still had bullets for it. Intact bullets were worth their weight in gold—because no one ever gave them up, and there was always something to shoot, whether it be one of the walking dead or a raider.

The comedian leaned against one of the sparse trees that jutted up from the interior of the town. The back of his fingerless gloves felt cool as he pressed his forehead to the leather.

As his bleary eyes scanned the town for some sort of escape, he noted that all of the citizens had shown up. The goofy looking boy with two tongues stood next to a man whose face was so dirty the comedian couldn't tell if it was grime or actual shit on his face. The grimy man put his arm around the boy's shoulders in a comforting manner, but he didn't seem to notice. He was too busy sniffing the fingertips of the mannequin hand. The comedian didn't want to know where those fingertips had been. In his other hand, the father held a cruel bit of rusty metal. Its jagged edge would open a man up easy enough, and if the wound didn't kill him, the tetanus would.

The comedian's stomach heaved, and he lost track of the words that Sheriff Eldoon spoke. The sounds of his own retching drowned out the sheriff's voice. When it seemed half his insides lay in the dirt, he looked up to find the entire town looking at him. Spots swam in his eyes, and he was too far gone to sense the danger he was in. He must have drowned his famed sixth sense. "What it is it?" he slurred, wondering if maybe he had farted when he was throwing up.

No one said anything. They stared at him like bored school children in a museum, back when there had been such things. For a second, his vision lit with a thousand stars, and then everything went black.

Chapter 8: Vengaboys and Spankings

The comedian's dreams were green and horrid, just like the Squirmgrass Ale he had pounded. *How long ago was that? Weeks? Days? Hours?*

His head floated and ached, and when he looked down, he found his body had followed him, floating into the air, hanging loosely from his neck. He climbed higher and higher in the sky. An airplane shot past him at 500 miles-per-hour, buffeting his weightless body and spinning him around until he threw up some more.

Some more? I don't remember throwing up.

That's because you're unconscious, Oddrey said.

The comedian turned to his right, and he smiled upon seeing Odd floating in the air next to him. Her hair floated behind her plastic face as if they were falling, but as far as the comedian could tell, they were maintaining their altitude.

"You're unconscious," he said.

All doll heads are unconscious.

"I hate you!" But he didn't. He loved Odd. She was so weird, so joyously glib. She said the funniest things.

"Wait, was that an airplane? Where am I?" The comedian finally took in his surroundings. Below him the world spread away, smaller and more put together than he had remembered it. On the ground, he spotted small silvery shapes travelling upon grey ribbons through fields that looked like patches of a quilt. *Cars. People. Roads.*

"It's beautiful."

It's a lie.

"Lie or not, I love it." Tears came to his eyes unbidden, only to be blasted away by the swirling wind. The sun shone pure and bright, warming his skin. He craned his head to the left and spied a city, tall skyscrapers still intact. Nowhere did the dead roam. Nowhere did cracks in the earth emit demons. Nowhere did clouds of radiation drift dangerously across the landscape. Everything was perfect. Maybe she was still there.

Dead, Oddrey said.

"What?"

I didn't say anything.

Dead. The word came again, but it wasn't Oddrey speaking it.

Suddenly, as if the hand of God had swatted him, he was knocked from the air. He plummeted to the ground. A bright light appeared in the corner of his eye, and as he fell to the earth, a hundred others like it appeared, arcing through the sky, tracing the curve of the earth. They moved faster than him, and as he continued his slow descent to the ground, the missiles made contact with their targets, blooming into nuclear mushrooms. The air vibrated around him. A cloud of super-heated atmosphere enveloped him, the last hot breath of a dying planet. He sweated as the mushroom clouds pushed into outer space. Buildings, tall and fragile, crumbled in clouds of dust as the earth shook from the assault of man.

Far below, a woman looked up at him, her mouth wide open in a terrible scream.

"Get out of the way!" he yelled.

But she didn't move, and he landed on her, crushing the life out of her.

He was still screaming when he woke up.

****

"Hello, sleepyhead."

The comedian recognized the voice of the man. This was the man who had been screaming about huffing and puffing and blowing doors down. This was the hack. He had killed men for less.

When he opened his eyes, he found it was still dark outside. Christmas lights, running off a chugging and smoking generator allowed him to see his captor. The man was a giant. His muscles glistened, shiny and wet. He suspected that this was on purpose. He bet that if he reached out and poked the man's giant, naked pectoral muscle he would find it was slathered in Vaseline. It wasn't hot enough to be covered in that much sweat, and the man wore hardly any clothing, just two leather bandoliers crisscrossed across his chest, and a pair of leather pants that strained against his massive quads.

Vanity. This was a vain man, someone who could be played.

As the comedian sat up, he noticed for the first time he was in a cage, built low to the ground so he couldn't stand up, even if he had wanted to. It was more like a kennel for a large dog than a prison cell. His head felt like it was going to split open, and he swore to himself that if he ever got out of the cage, he would never drink Squirmgrass Ale again.

"Who are you?" the man asked.

"No one," the comedian said, his head leaning against the cool bars of his cage.

"No one?" The man smiled.

Though black spots still swam in his vision, the comedian forced one eye open. His face looked like a ball covered in fur. Though the top of his head was bald, his wispy, brown facial hair covered every inch of his cheeks. The hair waved in the wind.

"Do you know who I am?" the man asked.

Everything would have been just fine if he knew the man's name, but he hadn't the slightest clue. He could not feed his captor's hubris, his pride. Instead, he attempted to appeal to the hack's obvious love of his body. "He-Man?"

"He-Man? What is a He-Man? This is like mister, misses, mix, yes? You think I am a He-Man. You think I am too good to love other men?"

Right then, the comedian didn't know what the hell he thought, and as he listened to the raider ramble, he realized the error of his ways. The man spoke with a faint foreign accent, and he seemed to be a couple years younger than the comedian. There was no way he would ever know about He-Man.

"I love who I want to, how I want to. I could be a She-Man if I wanted to."

"That's not what I meant."

"You don't tell me how to love. No one tells Joe LaBro how to love."

The comedian saw his chance. "You're Joe LaBro?" he asked placing the ring of familiarity on the name and making it sound as if he was known all over.

"You've heard of me, yes?" the man said. He smiled, and the comedian caught the faint shadow of fibrous meat between his yellow teeth. It was always the way.

"Oh, yeah, of course. Even two towns over, they've heard of Joe LaBro. They say you're the wildest, sexiest raider that's ever trod the rad zones."

Joe LaBro smiled at him, and he could tell that the man's ego was swelling. Unfortunately, the comedian spotted something else swelling underneath the man's loincloth.

"You're like little version of me. I call you Lil' Joe. You want to sleep with me? You make good little spoon."

"I can't. I'm married," the comedian said.

Joe LaBro reached down and pulled the comedian's arm through the bars of his miniscule prison. He held up his left hand and pointed. "No ring. You lie."

"I'm not lying," the comedian began, but then his protestations turned into strained yelps as Joe LaBro repeatedly slammed the comedian's twisted arm against the bars of the cell.

"You lie! No ring, no marriage. You lie to Joe LaBro. I show you what we do to liars. Radim, Pet, bring this man out of there. I will paddle his flesh until it is pink and the truth flows from his mouth."

The comedian had a moment to size up the two raiders, Radim and Pet. Radim was a wiry man, his arms covered with sores like tiny volcanoes. From each of these tiny volcanoes, yellow pus oozed like dull mustard. He was covered in slime, as if he too had covered himself in Vaseline at one point, forgotten, and then rolled around in the dirt.

Pet was one of those strange raiders that seemed to have used the end of the world to explore their sexual side. It seemed like half the raiders in the world could only find bondage gear to wear. Pet's outfit left little to the imagination, and the comedian wondered how, in this world, Pet could walk around with his butt cheeks flapping in the wind. Straps and buckles covered his body, and the comedian started to get a really bad feeling.

The two raiders threw open the cage, and he watched with greed as the key to the padlock disappeared down the front of Pet's corset. Despite being obviously stronger, the two managed to drag his weakened, hungover body from the cage. Even though he struggled and fought, he couldn't stop them from bending him over Joe LaBro's knee. With a metal-studded paddle that seemed more at home in a dominatrix's dungeon than a raider village, the raider boss began smacking the comedian on the ass while Pet and Radim held his arms and legs.

He jerked and cried out, from embarrassment and outrage more than pain.

Joe LaBro laughed, savoring his protestations. "Now you know why we're called The Flesh Paddlers!"

"You gotta be kidding me!" the comedian responded. But his voice was drowned out by the smack of paddle against his bare butt cheeks.

He didn't know how long the beating went on, but eventually, Joe LaBro tired of spanking the comedian, and the raider lord's lackeys dragged him back to his cage. Every muscle in his body ached, except for his ass, which had gone uncomfortably numb.

With his cage closed and locked, Joe LaBro strode over to him, and the comedian ignored the bulge in his leather pants.

"You're sick," the comedian gasped, too weak to put any real force behind his words.

"Thank you," Joe LaBro said, his voice dripping with sensuality. "Thank you so much for your sacrifice."

"Go fuck yourself."

Joe licked his lips and smiled. "What did you do to those people in Shithole that they were so quick to give you up?"

"I didn't do anything."

"Come now. You must have done something. We usually have to kill a couple people to get anything out of Shithole."

"I'm an outsider."

Joe smiled gently, and the comedian's suspicions were confirmed. Joe LaBro was almost positively insane.

"Tell me of the sights, outsider. Where did you come from?"

With feeling returning to his once numb backside, the comedian had no intention of offering anymore pleasure to Joe LaBro. But, on the other hand, he wanted out of his fucking cage. Maybe he could work a deal. "I'll tell you if you let me out of here."

This brought the smile back to LaBro's face. "A farmer does not make deals with the chickens. If I want your words, you will give them to me, or you'll face the paddle."

"Chickens? You're not gonna eat me, are you?"

"Look around, outsider. Do you see any crops? We're on a meat diet, and you're meat." Joe LaBro licked his lips and continued, "But you still look a little tough, like leather. Tomorrow, we'll tenderize the rest of your body. It makes the meat... sweeter. Tonight, we party!"

The massive man stood up then, turning on a leather booted heel. From somewhere in the raider camp, a second generator roared to life. Inky black smoke filled the sky. A horrid sound assaulted his ears, and as he covered them with his hands, he recognized it as music.

"The Vengaboys? Come on! They gotta have something better than this!"

Saccharine, pointless pop tunes assaulted him, and the sky grew orange and mottled as the sun came up. It had been a long night for the comedian, long indeed. With his hands firmly clamped over his ears, he passed out once more.

****

Sometime in the middle of the day, with the smudge of the sun beating down upon him, he awoke to find a set of piercing blue eyes staring at him.

"What are you looking at, freak?"

Pet didn't like that. Grunting shrilly, the creature grabbed the bars of the comedian's cage and shook them. The bars rattled, and the sound of metal upon metal was like a hot soldering iron being driven directly into the comedian's brain.

"Ok, ok. I take it back. Just keep it down."

Pet stopped his tantrum, and the comedian leaned his head against the bars, closing his eyes to block out the glare of the sickly orange sun.

His eyes snapped open as he felt a hand running through his hair. Pet, now inches from his face, was stroking him like he was a prized house cat. The comedian didn't know the last time he had experienced human contact that didn't involve his fist bashing into someone else's face. Something inside him stretched, and he realized that he was experiencing an emotion. Revolted, at himself more than Pet, he snatched at the man's hand and pushed it away.

Pet grunted, and his mouth opened for the first time to reveal a severed tongue and a handful of busted teeth. Quicker than a blink, Pet snatched Odd from the comedian's jacket pocket in retaliation for his rejection. The comedian's arm shot out like a cobra to snatch the doll head from Pet, but the wretch had already danced out of his reach.

"Give 'er back," he demanded.

Pet shook his head and danced across the dead grass.

"I said give her back."

In response, Pet moved the doll head in the vicinity of his rear end.

"Don't do it!"

Pet showed his broken-toothed smile, and then the doll head disappeared, right up Pet's backside.

"You're dead, Pet. When I get out of here, I'm going to do things to you that you wouldn't believe."

Pet twirled away kicking up bits of dust that most likely carried enough radioactivity to kill them all over time. But he didn't have time. When the sun got lower on the horizon, the raiders, all tuckered out from partying, would wake up hungry. They would come, and they would eat him. The only real question was, would they cook him while he was dead or while he was alive?

All around him, he saw boot tips and butt cheeks pointing up at the sky. The Flesh Paddlers, sick fucks, had partied all night, unleashing a cavalcade of obnoxious technopop that had tainted the comedian's dreams, maybe even his soul. Now, they all lay passed out wherever they had fallen. Some slept in the dirt. Others crashed in small hovels made from bits of dry-rotted wood and street signs. The haunting sound of a paddle smacking flesh still rang in his ears.

The comedian looked down at the dirt below him as if he could dig his way out, but his cage was complete. He was boxed in on six sides by stout metal bars that only showed small amounts of rust. He thought about trying to bend the bars, but unless the radiation had given him super-strength overnight, the bars would not give.

He licked his dry lips and leaned his head against the bars once more. It seemed like the only thing he could do was wait.

Chapter 9: The Cleansers

For Ajax, this raid had been a long time coming. No, not raid. That would make her a raider. This was a purge of chaos. She and the others were here to stop the spread of chaos, to keep order in the world so it didn't fracture further. The world was at the tipping point, teetering at the edge of a slope. If it fell, it would never make it back. That's what the Fury said at least, and the Fury would know better than her.

She wasn't a Reader, didn't know how to interpret the signs of the world. All Ajax knew was how to stop chaos in its tracks, and that's why they were outside the raider's settlement now. From the trees, she scanned the home of the Flesh Paddlers. For some time now, she had been hoping to discover their hideout, and here it was before her. Its walls were woefully pathetic, plywood and 2x4 supports. If she jumped in the air, she would be able to see over them.

When the good people of Shithole had sacrificed the outsider to the clutches of the raiders, she knew her chance was upon her. Armed with her mace, Ajax was ready to put an end to the chaos of the Flesh Paddlers.

The music had died off, fading away some hours ago. The sounds of yelping and flesh smacking had disappeared as well. She didn't know what they were doing to the man in there, and indeed, she feared he was a lost cause already. If they could save him, they would, but if he was dead, it was no big loss.

In other settlements, she had seen wanderers like him before, desperate men who stayed alive by exploiting the sweat and labor of others. They were agents of chaos in her mind, traveling from town to town, smuggling trouble in their packs. His death would be no great loss; it might even be a good thing. The loss of another agent of chaos might stabilize the region and keep it from plummeting into utter anarchy. The itinerant brought death and disease from one village to the next, and even if they were healthy, their lack of loyalty to those around them only led to more chaos and conflict.

A bird call shrilled across the compound, and the forest around her trembled in anticipation. But the forest would have no bird to snack upon because the bird call issued forth from the throat of Comet. The others were in position.

Ajax broke into a run, sprinting for a spot in the wall that looked ready to tumble to the ground should a stiff breeze come along. As she ran, her chainmail jingled underneath her cloak, her muscles bunching as she dashed for the wall. She yanked her mace from the loop on her belt, and without pausing, thundered through the plywood sheets of the raider den.

Plywood and 2x4's clattered to the ground amid a cloud of dust. A raider sat up just in time for his forehead to meet the harsh steel of her mace. The raider toppled over with a dent in his head. Around the camp, the alarm went up. "To arms! To arms!" they cried, even as Comet and Silver burst through the outer wall a few seconds later.

The end of her mace dripped blood as she let loose a triumphant laugh of challenge. The raiders, many of them still with drool running from their mouths, stumbled to their feet, hungover and still half-asleep. They would be no match for her. Raiders never were. The only reason raiders were a problem was because they had the numbers. Other than that, they couldn't fight for shit.

Even as she thought this, a raider wielding a mile-post sign with a razor-sharp edge took a swing at her. She stepped inside the arc of the swing and brought her mace up under the raider's chin. His jaw broke, and blood and teeth flew from his mouth. *No more eating human flesh for that one.*

A man wearing a white plastic mask with holes drilled in it ran at her swinging a wooden club wrapped in razor wire. The man's body was covered in pustules of disease. Ajax blocked his first swing, then brought her mace down on top of the man's head. His eyes rolled up as if he could see the damage she had done, and then he collapsed to the ground, dead.

Red rivers formed in the dust. Instead of soaking into the soil, the blood pooled on the ground. Even the earth itself wanted nothing to do with the raiders or their poisoned blood.

Then the largest raider she had ever seen kicked open the door to a ramshackle building. In his hands, he wielded a giant chunk of concrete with a steel bar sticking out of it. It reminded her of the frozen fruit pops they used to make back home, only a hundred times larger. He roared like an animal at Ajax, and she smirked in response, unintimidated. *Probably too stupid to think up anything clever to say.* That was always the way with raiders.

His body glistened in the orange sunlight, and the giant sneered at her, his broken teeth yellow and filthy. Ajax had never seen a raider this big. He was unnatural, perhaps some sort of mutation, a manifestation of chaos itself. Certainly, no normal human could ever grow to such a size. She reminded him of the Incredible Hulk, only, this guy wasn't green, and he definitely wasn't one of the good guys. His death would pave the Broken Path and restore order. Today was going to be a good day.

Leather pants creaked as his tree-trunk legs pounded across the ground between them. Snaked with veins, his bulging arms twirled the monstrous chunk of concrete as easily as a child playing with a baton. As the raider closed on her, he swung the massive chunk of concrete at her ribs. Ajax rolled out of the way of the blow and popped quickly to her feet. Dodging was her best course of action here as she wouldn't be able to block the force of such a swing with only her mace at her disposal.

Off to her left, a pile of bones in a gimp mask ran at her, a small knife in her hand. For the first time, she felt some sense of remorse for her actions. Life in a raider camp was no picnic for a woman. Of course, remorse didn't stop Ajax from aiming a two-handed swing right at the woman's head. Her attacker leaped into the air, the small, rusty knife poised for Ajax's face. Her leap ruined Ajax's aim, but the mace still connected, crushing the woman's windpipe instead of caving in her face. She collapsed to the ground, her feet kicking the dirt as she tried to breathe through her collapsed trachea.

"I'm gonna paddle you for days," the massive raider bellowed.

Behind the giant, Silver approached, his own blood-drenched mace raised over his bald head, ready to deliver a killing blow. Somehow, the raider sensed Silver's approach, and he spun, twirling the giant chunk of concrete with an ease that made it seem like it was made of Styrofoam. The rough concrete connected solidly with Silver's chest, and he flew ten feet through the air before he hit the ground, clutching at his smashed sternum.

The raider raised his concrete bludgeon in the air for a killing blow, and Ajax darted in, connecting solidly with the back of his knee. Hamstrung, his massive leg crumpled underneath him, and Ajax popped to her feet, readying herself for another swing. Her mace stopped in mid-swing, connecting with the chunk of concrete. Somehow the raider had gotten it up at the last second, otherwise, she would have bashed his brains in.

Sounding like a mutated badger, he growled at her. That's all he really was—an animal, a rabid beast that needed to be put down for the good of the world. With a hand like a catcher's mitt, the raider shoved Ajax backward and then lifted himself to his feet. Hobbling on one leg, he stood, and then Comet appeared, streaking silently across the encampment.

Comet's mace dripped with blood and gore as well. They had each done well, bloodying their weapons and striking a blow for order. A cut swerved from her eyebrow to her cheek, and her blood glowed a muted red in the filthy glare of the sun. Like a panther she streaked, silent and quick. When Comet was within striking distance, she leapt into the air, baring her teeth in a wicked grin. Comet's mace smashed against the back of the raider's head, and he toppled forward into the dirt with a soft grunt. The massive chunk of concrete stood on its end, a monument to the raider's death. It would make as good a tombstone as anything.

Gasping for breath and quaking with adrenaline, Ajax looked for her next opponent, only to find there were no more raiders left standing. Everywhere, dying bodies lay strewn upon the ground, breathing their last breaths or bleeding their lives away into the baked and compacted dirt.

In a corner of the compound, she spied some movement.

"Hey," a voice called. "Hey, over here."

Ignoring the voice, Ajax rushed to Silver's side. He lay still on his back, blood running from the corners of his mouth. She squatted next to him, softly placing a hand on his sternum. Even that amount of small pressure caused him to grunt in pain, and she hastily removed her hand from his crushed chest.

"Are you ok?" she asked as Comet squatted next to her.

Silver simultaneously coughed and groaned in pain, flecks of blood arcing up from his throat only to come crashing back down upon his tan cheeks. "Can't breathe," Silver managed to utter.

111

"It's alright. We'll get you back to town, and you can heal up."

"I'm not gonna make it."

Ajax smiled down at Silver. He always had such a defeatist attitude. "We'll get you back to town. We'll see to that. Alive or dead, well, that's the real question, isn't it?"

Silver choked in laughter, and Comet looked at her with anger in her eyes. Ajax couldn't help it if she was the funny one.

"You suck," Silver moaned.

Together, Comet and Ajax lifted the broken Silver to his feet. He staggered, his massive weight pressing down on the women's small frames. If Ajax had been given the choice to carry a small cow or Silver, she would have chosen the cow, not that there were any left anymore... just the ones she had seen in children's picture books.

"Hey? You just gonna leave me here?" a voice called.

"The outsider," Comet said, a hint of annoyance in her voice. "Should we set him free?"

"I suppose so. Maybe he can help carry Silver back to Shithole."

Together, Ajax and Comet carried Silver to the edge of the raider's camp and leaned him against a wall. Ajax left Comet supporting the big man, and then she strolled over to investigate the cage and the man trapped inside.

The man looked like crap. Dark circles ringed his eyes, and his hair was mussed, bits of dead straw tangled in the medium-length strands.

"Well, howdy miss. Thanks for killing those raiders. I would have done it myself, but..." The man looked apologetically at the bars of his cage.

Ajax bent down and pulled on the padlock. It didn't budge. "Hmmm... locked. Sorry, vagabond."

With that done, Ajax turned to leave, but the man called out to her. "I know where the key is!" Despite his

112

efforts to hide his panic at being left behind, strands of his fear still bled through in his voice.

She had always been able to pull hidden meanings from the words that people said. The Fury said it was her gift, called it the ability to "read between the lines," though Ajax had no clue what that actually meant. Right now, it meant that the man in the cage was scared out of his mind of being left for dead, though he didn't seem to want to show it.

"Where is the key?" she asked, feeling slightly put-upon. She could almost smell the fear coming off the man. He was pathetic. When she had first laid eyes upon him, she had failed to see through his ruse. At first, she had taken him for a plain bounty hunter, but as she and the others had watched him play Bosses and Offices in the bar, she had seen him for what he was—just another desperate man trying to play at having a life.

He was the type of person she was fighting to save. She would put things in order, and then the man wouldn't have to be so desperate. He wouldn't have to live in fear. He could settle down and stop drifting from town to town without the fear of losing something he loved.

"That one, over there, the one with the buttcheeks and the blue eyes. It's in his corset."

Ajax turned and strode in the direction the man pointed. Squatting over a lithe form in the dirt, she easily spotted the blue eyes the man had mentioned—as one of them was hanging out of the poor soul's face by its optic nerve. Silver had really done a number on this one. For a second, a thought flitted across Ajax's brain, and she wondered if what they were doing was actually good, but the thought fled as quick as it came. *Of course we're good.*

She reached down the front of the corpse's corset, her fingertips sliding across smooth, cooling skin. Her fingertips brushed against something metal, and Ajax clasped it in her hand and pulled it free. With the key

113

pinched between her thumb and forefinger, she stood and turned to address the wastrel in the cage.

"Will you help us carry our friend back to town?" she asked.

"You betcha," the man said, a toothy, wolfish smile spreading from ear to ear. She heard the truth in his words, and something else that she couldn't quite name.

The feeling of his words made her queasy, but she bent down and placed the key in the lock anyway. The padlock fell away with a click, and the man in the cage scrambled out like a clumsy dog. He stood, knuckling his back, and then he walked over to the body of the key-bearer. The man glared down at the corpse, and then he pushed it over on its side and began to… dig in it. Ajax turned away wondering if she had made a horrible mistake in freeing the man. *Have I just loosed a madman upon the world? Some vengeful pervert?*

Ajax heard a dull thump she recognized as a boot impacting limp flesh. "That's for touching me." Another thump. "And that's for stealing Odd." A series of thumps that sounded so violent that Ajax couldn't help but turn and see what the man was doing.

Clenched in the man's hand was a brown doll head. The body at his feet was smashed in ways that it shouldn't have been. The raider's legs and arms were broken. Its face was no longer recognizable, and the animal sneer on the man's face was sure to haunt her dreams.

"And that's for shoving Odd up your ass, ya fucking savage. There's rules out here. You don't stick someone's friend's head up your ass. You just don't. Like, no one needs to say it; everyone just knows it, except you."

The man wiped some filth from the doll's face, and Ajax saw that the dollhead's skin wasn't actually brown. Then it dawned on her exactly what she was seeing, and why the man had been kicking the corpse in the first place.

"Are you ready?" she asked the man, eager to get Silver back to Shithole.

"Yeah. Let's go." The man positioned the doll head so it hung from his pocket. Then he turned and strode past Ajax as if nothing had happened.

Walking confidently and upright, the man only came up to her shoulder as he passed her by.

As they approached Comet and Silver, the man turned and looked at her. "This the guy?"

Ajax nodded.

Comet introduced herself and held out her hand. The drifter just looked at the hand, and then held up his own. "Got raider shit on my hand." Comet let her hand drop, and they stood smiling at each other awkwardly.

"I'm Ajax."

The man looked at her, a quirk of a smile on his lips. "Comet, Ajax? Wait. Don't tell me—this guy's name is Mr. Clean."

"His name is Silver," Ajax corrected.

"That's a shame," the man said. "Bit of a missed opportunity if you ask me." The man ducked under Silver's arm, and Comet's face immediately appeared less strained. "Well, shall we hit the road?"

Ajax nodded, not failing to note that the man had never actually introduced himself. *Was he hiding something?* Her gut said yes, but it also didn't tell her if whatever he was hiding was good or bad, so she ignored the feeling… for now.

"You could call yourselves The Cleaners."

"That's a terrible name," Comet said. Silver groaned in agreement.

"Cleansers then," the man said.

"It's only one letter difference," Ajax said. "And it's still terrible."

115

The man muttered something under his breath, and Ajax could just barely make out the words. "You can call yourselves the fucking Critics then. Ungrateful..."

The words trailed off into quiet, and Ajax scanned the surroundings for any threats, while a parade of whispered rumors and legends about a mysterious drifter ran through her mind. It wasn't a long way back to Shithole, but any journey outside of a city's walls felt long enough.

Chapter 10: The Game of Bones

At the entrance to Shithole, the comedian stood behind the Cleansers, his head down. As they approached the gate, he heard Sheriff Eldoon call out, "Who goes there?"

Your fucking death. The comedian smiled on the inside.

"It's Ajax, Comet, and Silver. Silver's hurt."

Shithole opened up wide, its brown gate swinging outward and the pungent smell of the town wafting over them. Out squirted Sheriff Eldoon to help carry Silver inside.

The comedian lifted his eyes and made eye contact with the sheriff, and he felt a small sense of satisfaction as the man's eyes saucered at the sight of his face. But then the sheriff turned and helped carry the big man inside the town.

No one stopped the comedian from entering the town that had given him up for dead. He wished they had. He would have liked to have seen at least one person try at least, one of these shitty little villagers. But no one did.

The comedian's first stop was the merchant's stall. Even though he was wearing his busy-looking mask, the comedian could sense the surprise in his body language as his hands and shoulders tensed up.

"Where's my shit?" the comedian asked.

"Haha! This is Shithole, all we have is shit. You're going to have to be more specific than that."

This was the wrong thing to say to the comedian. Reaching across the table, he yanked the merchant off his feet. The table tipped to the side and his baubles and trinkets rolled onto the packed dirt. The comedian pulled the merchant closer and with one hand ripped the helmet from his head.

Underneath, the merchant half-grimaced/half-smiled at him. He had a soft face, not the face of a murderer. His head was bald, and his eyes were kind. The comedian pulled him close so the merchant could see his own eyes were anything but kind.

"I'm gonna ask you one more time. Where's my shit?"

From the darkness of the stall, the comedian sensed the crossbowman taking aim. His sixth sense rang like a fire bell. He thought he could hear the tendons in the assassin's hand tense, and when he couldn't stand it anymore, he swung the merchant between the crossbowman and himself. The crossbow's string twanged, and the merchant's kind eyes turned into eyes of agony as he grasped at his right butt cheek.

"Oh, she got me. Got me right in my byoo-tocks." The comedian threw the injured man to the ground and sprinted to the back of the merchant's stall. There, he spied a slender form trying to reset the crossbow's string for another shot. With one meaty fist, he delivered a backhand to the skinny assassin.

The woman groaned in pain and crashed against the wall. She landed in the dirt, her toes to the sky, and she was still. The comedian picked the crossbow off the ground, easily cocked the string and placed another bolt in the flight groove. With the crossbow once again ready to deal death, or a butt puncture, he stood over the prone form of the merchant.

"Where's my shit?" he asked.

The merchant pointed into the shack. "Fake wall," he groaned. "Behind the American flag."

"Fake flag, too," the comedian said. He stepped into the shadows of the merchant's cabin. The faint orange light from outside seemed to bounce off the faded rectangle of the American flag, a forgotten relic of a failed experiment. Where before you would see every doughy, round, white

118

person flying the thing, now they were mostly hidden away or burned to ash. Not even the promise of Uncle Sam could stop the apocalypse, and the survivors hadn't forgotten that. Sure, you'd find a true believer out there every once in a while, talking about republicans and democrats, talking about how America would come back. But the American Dream was dead, always had been.

No one pulled themselves up by their bootstraps anymore, which had always been a physical impossibility in the first place. Now, people were lucky to have boots. The leather in shoes was not impervious to time, to the elements. Leather could rot just like flesh, and if you got hungry, boiled leather offered a scant amount of nutrition.

Snatching the flag off the wall, he tossed it on the ground. He didn't do it out of spite, out of hatred for a country that had once claimed to be the best in the world; he did it because the flag didn't matter. It was a symbol of nothing. It had never actually meant anything to begin with. It was just some stars, some stripes, some cloth.

Behind the flag, the wall seemed solid. He ran his hands along the edges looking for a hidden catch, and then he found it, a faintly recessed piece of wood. He pushed on it, and a small door swung open. In the tiny space, he found his sword, his backpack, and lo and behold, his goggles were in there too. That meant Mugs at *The Upper Decker* had been in on it as well. No wonder he had gotten so tanked the night before; Mugs must have slipped a little something in his drink.

"What did Mugs get out of the deal?" the comedian called to the merchant.

"Actual mugs."

The comedian nodded. That seemed like a fair deal.

The comedian threw on his backpack, his sword, and his goggles. Then he turned to leave. As he passed the merchant, he tossed the crossbow on the merchant's chest.

119

"That's a coward's weapon," he said as he turned and headed for the bar.

The villagers in the town eyed him differently now. They were not curious about him anymore. They were cautious. But they wouldn't start shit. No one risked their lives on a whim in a village. None of these people would be alive if they had that sort of personality trait. Whims got people killed in this world. But they watched him just in case, to see if he was hellbent on revenge.

It turned out he wasn't, which surprised even himself.

He passed a dingy tent constructed of old canvas. A red plus sign had been painted on the side. Outside, Ajax stood watching him, her green eyes seeming to float in mid-air due to the band of black and red facepaint that ran across her face. Her arms were crossed, and he could see a small cuff of silver chain-link armor peeking out from under one of her sleeves.

He had heard of people like her before, but only in passing. People in villages whispered about her kind, though none had claimed to ever see one. They were called Chicken Kickers, agents of good. They were like some sort of jumped-up vigilante squad. He'd heard tell of maces and chain-link armor, but until now, he had believed the rumors to be just that. Now he had proof.

Ajax glared at him, her gaze stalking him across the compound. Inside the tent, he could see the bottoms of Silver's boots.

He better hope he doesn't need any surgery, Oddrey said.

She was right. Surgery was a death kiss in the wasteland. The number of people left who could pull off something like surgery probably numbered in the tens, and he doubted a town like Shithole would possess such a treasure. Still, people remembered surgery, remembered the basics they had seen in TV shows they had consumed when

120

people had the luxury to sit on their ass and do absolutely nothing but stare at a box. They still remembered the word sterilized, liked to scream the word *STAT* at each other… and they knew how to sew skin, crooked and jagged. But in the end, infection always seemed to take those who went under the knife. Antibiotics were a thing of the yesterworld. He hoped Silver didn't need surgery either. Better to die on your feet than from unseen germs.

Giving Ajax a mocking salute, he continued on to *The Upper Decker*. He still had business with Beatums, and the motherfucker better still be there.

As he approached the bar, his stomach fluttered with butterflies. Another game. He was down one to nothing now… and he needed to win both of the next two games, or he'd never find Cheatums.

The patrons of the bar jumped as he kicked open the batwing doors—everyone except for Beatums.

"Mugs!" he yelled, and the large man with the show muscles wrung his hands, a look of fear on his face. That was good enough revenge for the comedian. Let everyone see how big a coward the man actually was. "I'm starving. Get me some food. I figure you owe me for all of those fancy mugs on your counter."

The bartender nodded and rushed from the building. At the rickety poker table in the center of the bar, Beatums sat, his eyes hidden by the green lid of his visor.

"So you had Mugs drug me, huh?"

"Wasn't not in the rules."

"That's a double negative."

"Double negatives are just reverse yesses. Ain't nothing wrong with that."

The comedian grabbed a chair and flipped it so the back rested against the rickety table. Then he straddled it and plopped down. Barely containing his rage, he leaned in close, and Beatums raised his head to stare the comedian in the eye. He had to hand it to the man; he had some salt in him.

"I'm no whiner, so I'm not going to accuse you of cheating. You won fair and square, and you get to pick the next game. So what's it going to be?" *Please be arm wrestling. Please be arm wrestling. Please be arm wrestling.*

Beatums reached into the inner pocket of his fur-lined jacket and pulled out a reddish-pink, rubber ball. At first, the comedian mistook it for a clown nose, and he almost laughed and said, "You must be joking. No one alive can beat me at clownin'." But, as Beatums bounced the ball off the table… he knew what he was in for.

"Knucklebones? You wanna play knucklebones?"

"I want to win knucklebones, not play it, ya peacock."

"Well, if you want to win, you better find someone else to play, because there's no way I'm losing."

Beatums smirked at the comedian, and they walked outside just as Mugs came scooting across the compound with some sort of grilled animal hanging from his hand. The animal was small enough that the comedian didn't bother to ask what it was because the answer would only kill his appetite.

Mugs held the creature up by the legs, and the comedian took it from the man. "I'll also take a pint of your finest, non-drugged ale, Mugs."

"You got it," the big man said, all smiles and hop-to-it-like.

Beatums stood, his hands in the pockets of his jeans as the comedian wolfed down the small creature while never taking his eyes from the man. He spat the small bones out on the ground. From the corner of his eye, he saw the mannequin arm kid lick his lips. If he hadn't been in the middle of an epic stare-down, he would have looked down and kicked the bones in the boy's directions. Sucking the marrow from a tiny creature was one of the few treasures left to people in this world.

When he was done, he tossed the mostly meatless carcass of the quadruped in the kid's direction. It landed with a thump in the dirt, but that didn't stop the boy from scooping it up and going to town.

"Jesus, that kid's hungry," Beatums said.

The comedian didn't turn his head to look. He wouldn't give Beatums the satisfaction of winning the stare-down. "Oh, is he? I wouldn't know. I'm too busy staring into the eyes of a loser."

Around them, the village had gathered in expectation of a legendary showdown. The comedian looked forward to providing them one.

Mugs brought his beer, and the comedian held out his hand without looking at the man. The bartender placed the mug in his greasy hand, and he tilted it back gently, still maintaining eye contact with Beatums. It was the slowest beer chug of his life. When he was done, he handed the empty vessel to Mugs, burped, and patted the sides of his belly.

"Well now, that was fantastic. You guys in Shittown really know how to treat a man. You know, when there aren't raiders around." Some in the crowd let their heads droop at the insult. Others pretended as if they hadn't heard exactly what the comedian said.

"It's Shithole!" Yokel yelled from the back of the crowd.

The staring contest continued.

"You'll never out-stare me," Beatums said.

"Let's play," the comedian said.

"Stump!" the two men yelled at the same time, their competitive juices in full froth.

Sheriff Eldoon appeared with a wooden stump in his hands. He ducked low so as not to interrupt the staring

123

contest and placed the chunk of wood between the two men.

The comedian reached out and ran his hands across the surface of the stump. It was nice and level, perfect for a good game of knucklebones.

"Bring us the bones!" Beatums called, and the merchant, still limping because of his punctured left buttock, pulled a cloth bag from around his neck. He untied the drawstring and dumped knucklebones out onto the stump. From the sound, the comedian knew that these were true knucklebones, the remnants of some child's once flesh-covered digits.

"Rules?" Beatums asked.

"If the ball bounces higher than your head, it's a disqualification."

Beatums smiled. "Right. If you drop the ball, you're out."

"No outside interference."

"No inside interference," Beatums countered.

"What—what does that even mean?"

"Don't know. But it'll be good not to have it."

"You wanna start at one?" the comedian asked.

"Why not? Let's give 'em a show. Loser's first." Beatums bounced the ball off the stump, and the comedian snatched it out of the air before it hit him in the face. Unfortunately, the action caused him to blink, and Beatums smiled.

"Lucky, we weren't doing a staring contest for the second game."

"Ooooooooh," went the crowd like a classroom full of children who had just heard the teacher burn a student.

"Yeah, well, maybe for the third game, my punctilious little Muppet."

"What's punctilious?" mannequin kid asked, but no one seemed to know.

The comedian felt the rubber ball in his hand. It was fashioned of smooth, firm rubber. It had a good amount of heft to it, and a small ridge of rubber stood out, marking the seam of the mold in which the ball had been cast, probably in a third-world country that no longer existed. He'd give anything to be living in a third-world country right about now.

"You mind if I have a couple practice bounces?" he asked.

"Boo! Get on wiff it, wastelanda!" crowed an elderly woman in a perfect wasteland accent.

The comedian, never one to disappoint his audience… wait, no that wasn't true. Whatever. The comedian nodded his head. "Goin' for one," he said. Then he took a deep breath and bounced the rubber ball off the stump. As it rose in the air, he reached down and snatched one of the knucklebones with his hand and then caught the ball before it had even begun its gravity-fueled descent.

"Not bad," Beatums said. "You got a little fox in them hands."

The comedian returned the knucklebone to the stump and handed Beatums the ball.

"But check this out," Beatums said. He bounced the ball off the stump and spun in a circle quick as a whip. His hand shot out like a striking cobra, and he pulled a knucklebone free, pinched between his thumb and forefinger. At the last second, he turned his hand, and let the ball land lightly on the back of his palm.

Oohs and aahs went up from the crowd, and Beatums graced the comedian with another cocky smile.

"Gimme the damn ball," the comedian demanded.

They moved quickly then, bouncing the ball and snatching up knucklebones. After each round, they increased the number of knucklebones they needed to grab by one. It didn't become difficult until the fifth round. The comedian bounced the ball and scooped his hand sideways

125

across the stump. The padded palm of his fingerless glove caught on the grain of the wood, and he almost fumbled the fifth knucklebone as the rubber ball made its descent.

He managed to snatch it at the last second, and then he turned his hand, sliding it underneath the ball just before it contacted the stump.

"I almost had you, wastelander."

"But you didn't," the comedian said.

As Beatums took his turn, scooping up knucklebones with ease, the comedian removed his fingerless gloves, exposing pale skin where his glove protected him from the sun.

"Ready to go to six?" Beatums asked.

"I was born ready, you pompous loaf."

"Well then how about we skip right to seven?"

A gasp went up from the crowd. "Seven knucklebones!" Yokel crowed. "It cain't be done!"

Beatums smiled, playing up to the crowd. "Not by this lead-handed cuss of a man. But I myself, I've gone all the way to nine before."

Doubt crept into the comedian's brain.

He's full of shit, Odd said.

But the comedian wasn't so sure.

"Let's go to seven." His pride was on the line.

"Loser's first," Beatums responded.

The comedian took a deep breath. At that moment, he felt like Indiana Jones about to replace a gleaming golden skull with a bag of sand. He hefted the rubber ball in his hand.

"Anytime, drifter."

The comedian ignored the gambler's barbs, and then he bounced the ball off the stump. With his right hand and its strange pastiche of tan and pale skin, he swept his hand across the stump, his skin rasping across the rough wood. The knucklebones rattled as they slid across the wood, pushed along by the skin of his bare palm. When he had

126

seven, he closed his hand around them, and squeezed his hand into a fist. He moved his clenched fist under the descending path of the ball, turned his hand sideways, and allowed the ball to balance on the side of his fist. It looked like he was holding a red snow cone in his hand.

A roar went up from the crowd, and Beatums looked from side to side. It was a new experience for him, seeing the folks of a village root for someone besides himself.

"How 'bout them apples?" the comedian jeered.

"Those are knucklebones, not apples," the mannequin kid admonished.

The comedian placed his bounty of knucklebones back upon the stump. Next, he bounced the rubber ball hard off its surface. Beatums reared back as the ball headed straight for his face but he managed to catch it before it struck him in the eye.

"Your turn, stretch," the comedian said.

Beatums was shaken. He hadn't expected the comedian to be able to pull off a seven-grabber, and now, it was time for Beatums to put his money where his mouth was. His mouth was currently on his face twisting about as he tried to envision the seven-grabber he needed to pull off.

The lanky man took a deep breath to steady himself, bounced the ball, and right as he went to sweep up knucklebones with his hand, a deep, comedic rumble filled the village. It sounded like a monster drowning in mud. Beatums heard it too, and his concentration was thrown off in just the slightest. A knucklebone tumbled off the stump and into the dirt.

He managed to snatch six knucklebones and the ball, but the game was already lost for Beatums.

As his defeat dawned on him, Beatums turned to the source of the sound. Sheriff Eldoon stood there, patting his belly and wincing apologetically.

"I'm sorry, Beatums. It's them damn navy beans. I tried to hold it in, but I couldn't hold it no longer."

Beatums let loose a primal scream as the comedian beamed from ear to ear.

The merchant swooped in and plucked the knucklebones off the stump. They were considered lucky, and anyone would kill for a set like the merchant owned.

The crowd, caught up in the contest, congratulated the comedian, patting him on the back. He shook them off and gave them menacing glares. He wasn't here for the adulation of simpletons, and he didn't trust the grimy, germ-covered hands of the villagers.

"Alright, Lose-ums. Are you ready for the third contest?"

Beatums spat into the dirt, and more than one villager looked longingly at the moisture as it soaked into the dust. "What'd you have in mind?"

"Cornhole."

Chapter 11: Cornholing in Shithole

"Absolutely not!" Sheriff Eldoon wailed in his weird country drawl. "There is no cornhole in Shithole! It's one of the rules! It's on the list. It is against the rules for you to cornhole with each other. Shithole is a wholesome place. I won't allow it!"

The comedian listened to the Sheriff's tirade, smiling inside. Outside, he kept his face impassive to let the Sheriff know how little he cared about the man's rules. Rules and the apocalypse didn't go together. The moment he saw the list of rules, was the moment he vowed to put the Sheriff's rules to the test. That the banning of cornhole was a rule the Sheriff had come up with specifically... well, that just made it all the sweeter.

He could have chosen something physical, something where he wouldn't have a chance of losing against the wiry Beatums, and while he would have been more than happy to do so for the second contest, he wouldn't stoop to such a cheap tactic to win the whole shebang. He was a man of honor—in his own way. He wasn't like a samurai or anything. There wasn't a specific code he lived by, but he did have his own nebulous code of conduct, though his rules seemed random at times. Mostly, he just didn't like being told what to do, and whenever anyone tried to force him one way, he would go out of his way to show the other party that they had no such power over him.

This was why he wandered—well, that and other reasons. But he would not live in a place where they constantly told him how to live his life.

The sheriff wound down, and everyone turned to the comedian, who had stood like a statue through Eldoon's passionate and, at times nonsensical, rant. With his mind elsewhere, the comedian had spaced out, so he had missed most of it. But he understood the gist. What it came down to was that Eldoon thought cornhole was a filthy game invented by the perverse. Like a tree stump politician, he threw out some sort of slippery slope argument that ended with everyone having a cannibal orgy. His last words were, "Do you want that? Do ya people? Everyone chewing on each other's genitals? Cause that's what's going to happen."

The comedian pulled his sword from his back and planted the tip of the massive blade in the dirt. "I'm gonna cornhole, whether you like it or not, Sheriff. Now, you can either stand to the side, or I can cut you in half. What's it going to be?"

The words were aggressive, tactless, but he had sailed past the point of caring some time ago. He almost had the information he needed, and he didn't plan to stick around after he got the scoop on Cheatums. This meant he didn't need to play nice anymore. Once he was gone, he didn't plan on returning to Shithole ever again. As the sheriff mulled his words, the comedian planned ways to kill the man, a thing he didn't want to do, but if he needed to cut the man in half, he would.

From the back of the crowd, he saw a blonde head appear. Green eyes swimming in face paint approached.

"What's going on here?" Ajax demanded.

The comedian eyed the mace at the woman's waist. It was little more than a sturdy doorknob affixed to a galvanized metal pipe, but it could do some damage. He had seen that back at the lair of the Flesh Paddlers. The woman had saved him, and while this may have meant something to someone else, to the comedian, it didn't mean a whole heck of a lot. Who was he that he needed saving? Who was she that she could play with his life like that? She had interceded once, but he wasn't going to let her do it again.

"Stay out of it, Ajax."

Sheriff Eldoon looked to the woman for help. "He's trying to break our rules. He wants to play cornhole."

Ajax seemed to relax. "So let him."

"But you don't know what it will lead to," the bald man whined.

"Where I come from, we have entire tournaments of cornhole during harvest time, and not once have we ever had even one cannibal orgy break out."

Equal parts elated and furious, the comedian swallowed his harsh words. *Where does Ajax get off interfering in my business?* Part of him didn't even want to play cornhole now. Ajax sucked. She was a black hole that took all the joy out of life for him. He hated her.

With his goal in mind, he stuffed his rage down inside. Beating Beatums was more important than venting his fury.

The town, with nothing better to do, rushed around prepping the game. They ripped the wooden seats from the latrines. The holes in the seats would make perfect targets. They set the boards against a couple of spare rocks to create an angled plane for the bean bags. For the bean bags themselves, a hoarding wench donated the temporary use of her secret stash of dry pinto beans. They sewed these up in burlap sacks, and then they were ready.

Staring each other down like fighters at a weigh-in, the crowd of villagers encircled the gambler and the comedian. Sheriff Eldoon stood off to the side his mouth downturned in a sour frown he'd worn ever since he had been overruled.

As far as the rules went, the game was simple. There were 10 innings, during which the players would alternate throwing bags. Any bag that stuck on the cornhole board was worth one point. Any bag that actually went through the hole in the board was worth three. At the end of the inning, after each combatant had pitched their four bags, the person with the larger score would have the smaller score subtracted from their own amount, and that would be the score for the inning. So if person A had ten points, and person B had eight points, the score for that inning would be 2 points for person A. Person B wouldn't get shit. Person B would be Beatums; the comedian envisioned it all in his mind.

He pictured himself being carried on the shoulders of the Shitholers, pictured himself giving the finger to Sheriff Eldoon and Ajax as they carried him through town. Finally, he pictured himself pressing his middle finger to Beatums' face and making a sizzling sound, as if he were branding the man, at which point, Beatums would give up all of the information that he had on his brother. It was going to be glorious.

Get your head in the game, Oddrey said.

"You gonna play or stare into space?"

The comedian shook his head, and came back to reality. "I'm waiting on you, Lose-ums. Losers first."

Beatums twirled the beanbag in his hand, showing off his manual dexterity. The comedian hated him for it. He copied the gesture in a mocking fashion, making it seem as simple as possible.

The gambler tossed his first bag into the air. It flew in a smooth arc, plopped onto the shithouse boards, and slid right into the cornhole.

"Beginner's luck," the comedian crowed as he copied the exact gesture and movement of Beatums. He too buried the beanbag in the hole. "Cornhole, motherfucker!"

Yokel, standing off to the side, sipping from a broken light bulb was the only person that cheered whenever the comedian scored. "Yeah, take that bag, Beatums. The comedian's all up in that hole."

It was nice to have a fan, although, every time Beatums scored, the noise was ten times louder, and the crowd would cast aspersions all over the comedian. Their filthy aspersions rained down upon him, covering him in their insipid passion, and he took those aspersions and made them his fuel. He gulped those greasy aspersions down, swallowed their bitter saltiness, and puked them back up as beanbag-tossing petrol.

"Byoo, you toss like a stumpy man!" one particularly cantankerous villager yelled at him. Her voice had the ring of Britain to it, but she definitely looked like some Midwest trash. She probably would have bled mayonnaise back when mayo had been readily available. He had no idea what a stumpy man was, but he didn't suppose it was a compliment. He rained another beanbag into the hole.

The two combatants traded score back and forth, neither taking a commanding lead. The crowd pummeled him with insult after insult, while they rained praise upon Beatums.

For the comedian, they called him things like a saucy-tosser and a fanny-flinger, real heartbreaking, soul-crushing stuff. For Beatums, they complimented his posture, the way he grew his hair, and the cleanliness of his index finger. The comedian couldn't help but feel jealous.

Finally, they came to the last inning with the score tied, and the comedian feeling less confident than when he had begun. The orange sun beat down upon him, and beads of sweat ran down his face. The air reeked of molten life, and the apocalyptic haze hung thick that day. The villagers, all crowded into one place, blocked any wind from reaching him, and their unwashed stench hung about his head so thick that he refused to open his mouth, for he knew he would taste their filth.

The comedian tossed his first bag of the inning, and it flew through the air, passing through the hole. Beatums threw his first, and it too sailed through, not even touching the sides of the board.

"You got this," Yokel called. "Beatums is gonna choke."

"I bet a can of gravy he won't," the merchant chimed in.

"I see your gravy, and I offer a gallon of my own special cocktail." Yokel laughed then, and his confidence filled the comedian with inspiration. His second beanbag arced through the air, and the crowd's collective mouths opened as they followed it, revealing teeth of all sorts of rotten shades, brown, yellow, and in one case, green. The bag landed on the edge of the hole. The comedian thrust his hips forward, as if that action could make the beanbag fall in.

Laughter went up from the crowd.

"You're a dead man, wanderer!" Beatums called. With seemingly no effort, Beatums tossed his second beanbag through the hole.

The comedian could feel the pressure now, tightening like a vice. His focus seemed to slip, and as he twirled the beanbag in his hand, it caught on his thumb and dropped to the ground.

"That's a toss!" Beatums called, pointing to the beanbag at his feet.

"Aw, come on. That wasn't a toss. It just dropped from my hands!"

"That's a toss, or my name ain't Beatums Winner Sterling!"

"That's not your fucking name! You were probably born a Harold or something," the comedian shot back.

"Nope, that's my actual name. If my birth certificate hadn't been burned to ash by a nuclear bomb years ago, I'd show you."

The comedian shook his head. "Yeah, well, whatever. That wasn't a toss."

Beatums spread his arms wide, looked around the crowd, and said, "Let's let the crowd decide. Was it a toss or not?"

134

The crowd sided with Beatums, yelling at the comedian, calling him a cheater among other things. The woman with the cockney British accent pointed at him and screamed, "Byooo, ya fucking tosser!"

"The crowd has spoken."

The comedian had no other choice. He had lost a toss and surely the game.

Beatums, a huge grin on his face, pulled his arm back for his third toss, and right at that moment, Sheriff Eldoon let loose another godawful blast from his posterior. The sound echoed across the village. A flock of two-headed birds alighted from the trees, and the guard on watch fell from the sky and landed in the dirt. Beatums, in mid-fling, pushed his beanbag wide, and it hit the dusty ground.

The angry gambler turned to the Sheriff and let loose a stream of curses so vile that the crowd leaned backwards, as if Beatums' vitriol could actually burn them.

The Sheriff, genuinely sorry, pleaded for Beatums' forgiveness. "I'm sorry, Beatums. I was tryin' to hold it in, but it got away from me. It's them damn navy beans. Kidney beans don't do that to me. Neither do lima, black, or green beans. Just them damn navies. You gotta believe me." The Sheriff fell down on his knees and crawled over to Beatums, tears running down his face. He wrapped his arms around the gambler's legs, and an embarrassed Beatums tried to shake the man off.

The comedian, a faint glimmer of hope kindled in his chest, took aim at the board. He pulled his hand back and let the beanbag fly. It flew on a straight trajectory, hit the beanbag still lying on the board and pushed it in, and then it hung there on the precipice. The crowd took a deep breath and everyone watched in silence. The entire wasteland went quiet, waiting to see if the bag would fall in.

Get in there, ya filthy beanbag! The comedian leaned forward, took a shallow breath, and blew outward.

135

His small breath floated across the clearing, making its way through the stench of the villagers, and it pressed ever so gently upon the dirty, burlap bag. It was less force than the flap from a butterfly's wings, but it was enough, and the bag inched its way into the hole, falling with the faint rasp of beans rubbing against each other. He was up 9-6.

Yokel stood up and yelled, pumping his fists in the air. "That's gravy, baby! Straight gravy!"

The crowd groaned, and Beatums looked at the comedian with hate in his eyes.

"This is it," the comedian called. "This is for all the marbles. If you don't make this, I win, and you gotta give me what I want."

"Shut up," Beatums called.

"Is that all you've got? Shut up? The great Beatums Sterling stands on the edge of defeat, and all you can say is shut up? I thought you were all wrists! You look like you drink from the shoulder to me!" the comedian spat.

A gasp went up from the crowd, and everyone fell quiet. Even Yokel, who had firmly been on his side for the entirety of the game, seemed taken aback.

"What? What'd I say?"

The crowd avoided looking at him. *Was the insult that bad? What does it even mean?*

Beatums stepped into the tosser box. No longer did he twirl his bag, he held his beanbag limply in his hand, and the comedian thought he could see the crystal glimmer of tears in his eyes. His arm rocked forward as he tossed the beanbag, and the entire crowd fell into a deep-hush. It arced through the air, passing enthralled faces, spinning end over end and creating a perfect twirling square as it traveled.

It landed with a raspy thump and sat dead on the end of the board.

"Yes!" the comedian yelled, pumping his fists in the air. He ran and grabbed Yokel about the waist and picked

136

him up in the air, screaming, "We did it!" over and over. The rest of the villagers groaned in disappointment before they turned and walked away. *I guess they're not going to carry me around the town after all.*

Beatums stood next to the cornhole board, his head down. The comedian had broken him in two, twain if you wanted to get fancy about it. He was no longer a man. The comedian had taken that from him.

As the comedian set the shaken Yokel down, the merchant pressed a can of brown gravy into the man's hand. Then the shopkeeper marched away, grumbling and making rude gestures in the direction of the comedian.

Still basking in the glow of victory, the funnyman leered at the merchant as he disappeared into his shop.

Sheriff Eldoon, sitting on his knees in the dirt, kept mumbling to himself, "This is why I wanted to ban cornhole. This is why it's bad. You never know what's going to happen. No cornhole, I says. No cornhole." His body shook as he sobbed, and he placed his hands to his face to hide the shame of his sorrow.

With a wolf's grin, the comedian strode across the distance between Beatums and himself. "Hey, Lose-ums. Time to pay up."

The beaten man looked up then, his mouth hanging open. "I lost. How the hell did I lose?"

"You know what they say about cornhole. Any given whatever-the-fuck-day-they-play-cornhole-on anyone can win."

Beatums looked off in the distance, and the comedian could tell that he had done more than just beat the man at a stupid game. He had crushed his identity, picked it up like a booger, rolled it into a little ball like the gross kid in 2nd grade, and flicked it off into the ether.

"But I can't lose. It's my name. I'm Beatums Winner Sterling, not Lose-ums Loser Sterling. That doesn't even sound good."

The comedian placed a conciliatory hand on the man's shoulder and said, "Hey, listen. I get it. It's tough not living up to your name and stuff, but how about you tell me where your brother is?"

"He's not here," Beatums said. The gambler was far away, as far away as a man could be and still be alive. Trapped in his mind, he replayed the toss of that final beanbag over and over.

"Yeah, I kind of figured he wasn't here. It's a small fucking town. I'm pretty sure I would have seen him by now. Why don't you try telling me something I don't fuckin' know."

"What do you want him for?" Beatums mumbled.

"None of your business. That wasn't part of the deal."

The man nodded sullenly, his chin drooping to his chest. "You want a rematch?" he asked, though the dejected tone of his voice hinted that he already knew the answer.

"Maybe in another time, another place, but I've already lost enough ground to your brother. I'm looking to get out of here."

At their feet, Sheriff Eldoon let loose a pained grackle squawk and rolled on the ground. "No cornhole. No cornhole."

Beatums took a deep breath, and for a second, he seemed more like himself. "You know, it always happens like this. Cheatums does something wrong, someone comes looking for him, and I save his bacon by gambling for his safety. I've never failed before. You know, I do believe that brother of mine might be more trouble than he's worth."

"That's great. So now's the part where you tell me where he went, yes?"

"I don't know why I even put up with him. He's never done anything for me. He's selfish, not good at anything except cheating. I guess my dad probably shouldn't have named him Cheatums. I mean—that's a

138

weird fucking thing to name a kid. How is a kid named Cheatums going to not grow up to be a huge cheater?"

The comedian smiled begrudgingly. It was a smile of tolerance. He had broken the man; there was no reason to grind the pieces into the dirt. "So, uhh, where is Cheatums again?"

Looking up at the orange sky, Beatums spoke in a distant voice, "Cheatums… he would always call me a shoulder drinker. Didn't matter how many times I bent at the elbow, he would say it right in front of everyone. It seems like my brother, when he wasn't cheating someone out of their beans, would spend the rest of his time tearing me down. A shoulder drinker—pfft, I never."

"West? South? He head to outer space?"

Beatums looked down, staring at the tips of his boots. "Well, never again. If Cheatums dips his stick in the fire, I'm not gonna be there to pull it out for him anymore."

"It's like you all speak a different language out here. Are you hearing me? Do the words I'm saying make sense to you?"

For the first time, Beatums looked at the comedian. "I hear you loud and clear. I'm just working through some stuff here."

"Well, do you mind doing it on your own time, after you've given me the information. I got a lot of catching up to do."

The lanky man nodded, and that old Beatums smile graced his face. "Cheatums left here the day he saw you arrive at the gates. He's got a couple days head start on you. He's heading to Ike."

The comedian had never heard of the town of Ike. "Where's that?"

"Oh, it's due east, into the Plains of Sorry."

"The Plains of Sorrow?"

"No, the Plains of Sorry. I'm not sure why they're called that. I never headed east myself, but Cheatums, when

139

he gets to runnin' he ain't afraid of nothing. It's funny how brave he is as a coward."

"What's Ike like?"

"Ya got me, stranger. I ain't never been there. Sometimes a trader from Ike will show up here, not very often, but he's always got interesting stuff to trade."

"How far away is it?"

"The traders say a week, if you know the way. If you don't know the way, it's gonna be a little bit longer than that."

"Ike, due east, about a week. Got it." The comedian clapped Beatums on the arm. "It's been a pleasure doing business with you. You're an elbow drinker in my book."

At this last parting, tears glistened in the man's eyes. Revolted, the comedian fled from him, his mind spinning at a thousand miles per. A week—a week of unknown road, a week out in the wilds where sometimes it seemed like the very planet itself wanted to kill you. He was going to need supplies, a week's worth, maybe two in case he got lost.

He had nothing to trade except for the items he would need in the wild, his sword, his backpack and its various contents, his clothes and his goggles. He was going to have to earn his pay. It was time to go to work.

Chapter 12: Priming the Pump

Despite his victory, the comedian was at a disadvantage. In addition to making a fool of the sheriff and the merchant, he had strolled into town and beaten one of their heroes. While he was fairly sure everyone could see the sheriff was an idiot, he knew his standing amongst the people of Shithole was not what it would have been had he showed up and done his show right from the get-go.

He was going to have to pique their interest. He had to prime the pump, get the wheels greased so to speak.

Yokel, a brown skin of gravy still ringing his lips, offered to help, and the comedian had no other option but to accept the strange man's aid.

"I need paper, cardboard, anything I can write on," he told the man. "You get that for me, and you can be my hype man when I put on my show. How's that sound to you?"

"You got it, babe. Anything for you."

The scrawny man's familiarity gave him the creeps, but he clapped Yokel on the arm and shot a winning, movie-star-style smile in his direction. Most people would do anything for that grin, and he knew it. It made him think that maybe he should smile more, and then he decided against it. You couldn't trust a man who smiled too often. That was a fact.

While Yokel was off finding something to write on, the comedian talked Sheriff Eldoon into letting him into the "guest quarters."

Once in the guest quarters, little more than a wooden room that smelled of shit and piss, he closed the door behind him. He set his gear on the floor, and from his backpack, he pulled a tiny scrap of broken mirror. With this, he set about cleaning himself up and making himself look presentable. With a damp rag, he wiped a week's worth of dust and sweat from his face. The rest of his body was clean, as were the clothes underneath his jacket. His jacket almost seemed magic in that way. It somehow kept him from collecting the filth of the road.

With a daub of his own spittle, he fixed his hair, making it look unkempt, but in a way that made people think of a model versus someone who had just rolled out of bed. Looks were important. No one wanted to see an ugly comedian… at least not the ladies and the guys that liked men. A real comedian had to look the part.

Smiling into the broken chunk of mirror, he presented his white teeth. White teeth were as rare as finding a working vehicle these days. People just didn't seem interested in keeping their teeth clean anymore. But he had the pearly whites, and they would wow people as much as his routine—more in some cases.

He cleared his throat and began working the kinks out of his show.

"So I say… no, that's not right." He paused, cleared his throat once more. "So I says… yeah that's the ticket. That sounds downhome, folksy."

They're not going to laugh at you, Odd said. *You're not funny.*

"Aw, you're just saying that because you know me. If you don't know me, I'm hilarious."

You think you're hilarious. You know you.

"Would you shut up? I gotta practice."

You're the only person in the world who practices sucking.

"I'm not practicing sucking… I… you know, just shut up, Odd."

The guest quarters fell eerily silent, and the comedian was alone with his thoughts for the first time in a long time. The clouds cleared from his mind, and all of the sudden he was the man he had always been, he was… a man with a name.

142

"I'm sorry, Odd. Come back."

Tears came to his eyes, and he forgot his comedy routine completely. "Please come back." Silence, cold and brutal, assaulted him. He looked at his hands and saw the blood on them. He tried to wash the blood away with his tears.

Crying isn't funny, Oddrey said.

"In the right hands, crying can split your sides open."

And you have the right hands?

"These are my hands, and they will do whatever I tell them to."

With Odd back, he felt safe again, confident. He ran through his routine, arguing with Oddrey about specific word choices, inflections, tones, and body movements.

In the middle of writing a song about the wasteland, someone knocked on the door.

Yokel stood there, his hair sticking up in the back like a child with a cowlick that couldn't be tamed. "Who're you talkin' to in there, mister?"

"None of your business who I'm talking to. Did you get the paper?"

Yokel pulled a rolled-up newspaper from his back pocket and handed it to the comedian. "You don't wanna know what I had to do for that."

"You're right. I don't wanna know. Get me some charcoal from the fire."

On a mission, Yokel headed off to do as he was told, and the comedian pondered what to write on the newspaper. With nothing in mind, he set about tearing the newspaper into hand-sized squares.

When Yokel returned, he snatched the charcoal from the man's filthy hands, told him to go practice his intro, and then slammed the door in his face.

"What should I write?" he muttered to himself. After a dozen false starts, Oddrey stepped in.

143

His only friend in the world spoke, and he listened, nodding. Then, with a steady hand, he scribed the words on the paper.

****

Yokel hadn't had a reason to live in years—maybe decades. Even before the world had burned, he had been on his way out. Every night, he expected to wake up dead... well, not wake up dead. You can't wake up dead. But he would uhh... he wouldn't be able to wake up.

Yeah... that's it. Yokel's thoughts swirled around in his brain, a jacked-up cocktail of randomness shot through with a faint tinge of purpose and old movie quotes.

"The intro!" he announced, finally remembering why he was hiding in one of shithole's many shitters. This one was seldom used as it was right next to the shitpile, and the stink was powerful, could suffocate a child in a matter of minutes. In his spotty memory, it seemed to him, it had at one point, or maybe he was just recalling a scene from Sleepaway Camp III. Through the moon-shaped cutout in the shitter's door, he could just make out the brown peak of the mountain the town added to every day. He imagined in a thousand years it would be an Everest of shit. But he wasn't adding to the pile right now. He was here for a different type of business—practicing his intro. He needed to get it right for the comedian, and he couldn't quite explain why. It was just something he needed to do. He needed to be needed, yearned to be useful as something other than a sacrificial lamb for raiders, which he knew would happen to him eventually.

When they had given away the comedian to the Flesh Paddlers, Yokel had felt equal parts relief and fear; relief they had gifted the comedian to the raiders instead of him, and fear that one day he would wind up being the one trussed up like a turkey and thrown outside the walls.

144

Along with the impending sense of doom that his own demise was marching purposefully in his direction, the comedian's abduction had also robbed Yokel of something he had thought lost in this world. Purpose.

The comedian didn't know it yet, but Yokel would be the best thing that ever happened to him. This he vowed from the bottom of his heart. After he delivered the world's best introduction, the comedian would take him on the road when he decided to leave. It had to happen that way. It was meant to be. It was fate, destiny… and another word that meant fate or destiny.

Oh, sure, he might die on the road, might get eaten by a zombie, might get devoured by a tree or fall into an evercrack and plummet into the center of the earth, but it would be an adventure, and he would be in control of his own life, insomuch as the comedian would probably choose where they were going, but it was still control on some level.

Yokel waved a monstrous orange fly out of his face and began practicing his lines. He started out shouting at the top of his lungs like an old timey carnival barker, but within the confines of the wooden outhouse, it was too loud. He modulated his voice, lowering the register, and he came off sounding more like a gameshow host the second time around.

"No, that's suck. It's garbage." He punched himself weakly in the face to get the blood flowing.

He tried a few intros with accents, a few without. He changed the words around, switching them in and out like Legos, popping them on and off sentences. An hour later, his throat was dry, and he had become light-headed. His Apocalypse Juice called his name, and he started to sweat as he tried to resist the urge to pop open another bottle of Xerex.

Yokel began to swoon in the shithouse, and he placed the back of a hand to his clammy forehead. Just as

145

he was about to pass out, someone ripped open the door, and Yokel screamed a shrill cry and dove against the back wall of the shitter.

As his eyes adjusted to the daylight, he saw the comedian standing there, a pile of newspaper shreds in his hand.

"Did you fall in? I've been waiting out here for like fifteen minutes. Everything alright?"

Sheepishly dusting himself off, he stood up and said, "Oh, yeah, I was just practicin' is all. I wasn't doing nothing else. Just practicing."

The comedian arched an eyebrow in Yokel's direction and said, "Yeah, whatever. Take these and pass 'em out."

"You got it, boss."

"I'm not your boss!" the comedian called as he walked away.

Yokel looked down at the newspaper squares in his hand. He used to know letters, used to know 'em real good. Hell, he had used to spell out movie titles on the marquee, but for some reason when he looked at the newspaper squares, he couldn't make heads or tails of what the words said. He even went so far as to conk himself in the side of the head with the palm of his hand, but all that did was make his eyes go blurry.

He played trombone with the paper squares, wondering if his eyesight had gone to shit at some point, but that didn't help either.

In the end, he decided he had forgotten how to read. He had never heard of anyone forgetting how to read, didn't even know it was possible. He thought it was like a bike or something, but he had never been really good at riding bikes either. He didn't like physical activity. Running was alright. It didn't require too much coordination, and no one ever saw you running and got jealous like they would if they saw you on a bike or a motorcycle, or an airplane, or a tractor. There were so many different types of transportation. Big ones, small ones. Wood.

Paper? He had seen paper airplanes before, and you could put an ant on them, so yeah, he figured paper was a form of transportation.

He looked down at the newspaper squares in his hand. *Oh yeah. Pass 'em out.* Yokel forgot the outhouse was elevated, and he fell straight out of it, landing in a puddle of bubbling mud. At least, he thought it was mud. With his face covered in bubble mud, he toodled around the village handing out the comedian's invitations.

****

Eddie Eldoon, the sheriff of Shithole, sat collapsed on the ground, mentally kicking himself. He had made a fool of himself in front of Beatums. And now Beatums was sure to leave, and he would never see him again.

His love would leave him.

Oh, Beatums had no idea that Eddie was in love with him, but he was—had been since the moment he and his toady big bro had walked into town. He remembered that day fondly. He still remembered the shine of the apocalypse glow as the sun peeked out from behind the clouds, illuminating the lanky gambler. He remembered Beatums smiling as his brother, always quick with something crass to say, made an unheard joke. That smile—it made his heart almost break in two.

He had been carrying that smile around in his pocket for weeks now, and now it was going to go away. He and his love for chili had been Beatums' undoing. As if in agreement, his guts roiled some more. He would never eat navy beans again. Any type of bean but navy. Navy beans were the work of Satan himself he decided.

As he continued feeling sorry for himself, Yokel came up and pressed something into his hand. He held it up to his weak eyes and was about to ask Yokel what it said when he saw Yokel had already moved on.

****

Mugs spat into the mug he polished. No one seemed to care about the spit except for the prissiest sort. But using water to clean out the mugs was a waste of water as far as most of the other villagers were concerned. He didn't particularly care either way, but a mug had to be clean, and his spit was the closest thing he had to dishwashing soap.

Besides, the alcohol sterilizes the glasses anyway. Right? Rags, the alcoholic in the corner, didn't care one bit. Hell, he would lick the glasses clean if Mugs let him.

As he looked across the taproom of his bar, he was struck by how quiet and somber it had become. For a while there, it had felt like a regular old bar, the type of place where people would come to swap stories, get shitfaced, and maybe head home with a random someone at the end of the night. But now that Beatums had been felled, it was as if the life had been sucked out of the town.

Despite their shitpile, despite the electricity, something was gone now, and the bartender knew he wasn't long for this town. He would be out there again, among the dust, among the cannibals, trying to survive on the bluff of an empty pistol and his bulging forearms. He would once again wander through towns where the bodies had been picked clean and the bones left to dry.

But that's the way the wasteland was, he supposed. Towns popped up like weeds, surviving for a bit only to be killed by a draught or to be eaten up by a two-headed deer that happened to pass by. Shithole would be gobbled up in no time, and all the residents would be cast to the winds, searching for some semblance of their former homes, searching for the lie of security. No place was safe really,

148

but for a while, he and the other Shitholers had been able to fool themselves.

He could craft alcohol out of anything… all he needed were some walls and thirsty patrons. He knew this town was moving on, and everyone felt it.

His head hung low as he spit in another mug and polished it clean. *I'm takin' my fucking mugs with me though.*

The batwing doors swung open, and it took all the effort he could muster to lift his head. He found Yokel standing there with a square of paper in his hand. The man, never one of his regulars, held the square out to him without a word. The bartender grasped it in his hand, read the words printed on the paper, and smiled for the first time that day.

****

The boy tested out the heft of the mannequin arm. He thought maybe the arm was getting lighter. *Maybe it's losing weight. Maybe I should feed it.* Only problem was there was no place to put the food. He lifted the fingers of the mannequin arm up to his nose and sniffed for the hundredth time. He didn't know what the smell was on those fingertips… it was kind of bad, but kinda good. One day he would know what that smell was, but for today, he would just enjoy it.

A man appeared. He had seen the man around town, but had been told to stay away from him by his da. His da was an important man around here. He knew the ways of making shit into energy, and though his da stunk to high heaven, he always managed to put food on the table. Maybe he could share some with the mannequin arm. He didn't want it dying. He knew people died easily.

The man broke his train of thought as he shoved a square of paper in his face. The boy snatched it, and the

149

man wandered off looking for someone else to hand paper to. The boy looked at the paper and wondered if perhaps the mannequin arm would like to eat it. He held the paper out to the mannequin arm, but it didn't seem to be hungry, and he couldn't figure out where its mouth was. Maybe it didn't like paper. He did, so he balled the paper up and popped it in his mouth.

The inks were bitter, old, but he liked the act of chewing. Yum. He smelled the mannequin arm's fingertips once more. What was that smell?

****

Ajax listened to Silver groan in the tent. Shithole's healer was really nothing to write home about, not that anyone was delivering letters anymore, but at least she had a place for Silver to rest, somewhere out of the burning sunshine and the burning rain.

If Ajax had ever had any doubts about the relationship between Comet and Silver, they had now been dispelled. Comet had eaten nothing since Silver had gotten injured. She stuck by Comet's side, wiping the sweat from his brow and fetching him anything he needed. The healer, a skinny red-haired woman with deft hands and a magic about her, had said Silver's chest was crushed, something anyone with two eyes could have pointed out. The injury could take weeks to heal according to the healer.

Comet had already approached Ajax about returning home to let Silver recuperate. But Ajax had other things on her mind. Whispered legends, snatches of daring-do rolled about in her head. She was curious. If Comet and Silver wanted to head home, she wouldn't stop them. It was not her place. Nor was it her place to follow them around like a puppy dog. She would let them go, but on their own. She had her own game to track.

150

Just then, a skinny man, smallish compared to Ajax, approached with something in his hands.

"Tonight only," the man said as he pressed a slip of wrinkled newspaper in her hand. He sped away from her, eyeing her mace with suspicious eyes. The man knew nothing. He had nothing to fear from her. He was harmless, an average towny, about as regular as an orange sky. Whether he knew it or not, he was a valued member of society and exempt from her justice.

Ajax, gifted in the art of reading, managed to puzzle out the smudged black letters. No smile crossed her face. She wasn't enthused or even curious. She just wanted to know more about her quarry. She would be in attendance. Ajax threw the cloak of her hood up over her head and ducked into the tent to talk to Comet and Silver. They would be parting ways soon.

****

The merchant swept his wares off his table and into a bag as soon as he saw Yokel stumbling in his direction. Though he had never caught the man stealing from him, he suspected Yokel had made a habit of bumping into his table and pocketing his goods for some time now.

"Fuck off, Yokel. Get away from here. Shoo! Shoo!"

"But I got something for ya."

"Just leave it on the ground and back away. You've got Buffalo fingers, and I want them as far away from my stuff as I can get them."

Yokel stared hard at his fingers for a moment, and then he balled the paper up and threw it at the merchant. It hit him square in the mask and tumbled to the ground. As he leaned forward, his mask bashed painfully against the table, but he still managed to snatch the paper ball off the ground with two fingers as Yokel disappeared. He

151

uncrumpled the scrap, his lips moving as he sounded out the words. When he was done, he took the paper in the back of his stall and found a large brick to set upon it. The newspaper still had one good side that someone could write on. It would be worth something to someone.

****

Beatums' saddlebags were packed and ready to throw over his shoulder. The road called. He hoped to catch up with Cheatums before the comedian did. If the comedian found his brother first, he was sure it would be the last encounter Cheatums ever had. He doubted the comedian just wanted to shake his brother's hand. Even if Beatums did find Cheatums, it would only be to warn him. He wasn't ready to go on the road with Cheatums again; he probably never would be, but the least he could do was give his brother a heads up.

He had made his living off reading people. In every town he stepped into, he knew exactly what people thought of him, could figure out what made them tick. Reading people had kept him alive and well-fed his entire life. Everything he sensed from the comedian screamed run the other way. The man was a lightning rod, and at any moment, lightning could strike. The comedian reeked of barely restrained violence, and though Beatums had come to understand that he really had no love for his brother, he didn't want to see him chopped up by the comedian's giant sword. If that meant his brother had to live life constantly on the run, then so be it.

For himself, he was ready to try something different. He was ready to make his own way and cut all ties with Cheatums. His days cleaning up his brother's messes were over. He would make his own fucking messes.

I just have to find the right place to set up shop. Any town with a large enough population will do. If it's got something to trade, then that's even better. He had always been able to make profit appear as if out of thin air. His uncanny luck often led people to believe that Beatums was a cheater just like his brother, but he had never needed to resort to such trickery to get what he wanted. That's why his loss to the comedian had been so devastating… that and the sudden realization his brother had never actually cared for him.

Cheatums, upon seeing the comedian at the gate, had taken to his boots. When Beatums had called after him, his brother had simply said take care of him. It was something he had been doing for years, and did his brother ever thank him? Did he ever change his ways? If anything, he became bolder, and whenever Beatums approached his brother about it, Cheatums called him names and told him to stop being such a baby.

All these years he had stood up for that piece of shit, and then, one day, a lowly drifter strolls into town and changes everything. No, the sooner he was away from the comedian, the better off he'd be. There was something about the man that didn't seem right, but Beatums couldn't put his finger on it.

He was just about to get Sheriff Eldoon to open up the gate for him so he could get a head start on the comedian when a shady looking character with sandy blonde hair and striking blue eyes came up to him. His shirt, about as filthy a rag as he'd ever seen, said, "God bless this Shithole." The letters were written in brown… paint?

The man held something out to him, and Beatums hesitated for a second. He didn't want to touch the man's filthy hand.

The man shrugged his shoulders and let the square of newspaper flutter to the ground. "Your loss," he said before he turned and walked away.

153

Beatums bent down and picked up the paper. The message read, "The comedian live. Tonight only."

Beatums had never been to a comedy show. He had read about them in books, maybe even seen some stuff when he was younger and the world hadn't burned yet. If there was one thing he knew about the wasteland, when it offered you up something good, that didn't threaten to kill you, you took it. Once the show was over, he could leave, not that he fancied leaving in the middle of the night.

He looked up at the sky. It was only a few hours until nightfall. He could maybe get a hand or two of poker in.

Chapter 13: The Show

The comedian set up his gear outside Shithole's walls. Once people saw all of his equipment and stage gear, there was always the small chance the residents of town would close the gates and kill him for his stuff. In order to avoid that, he needed an avenue of escape, and performing outside provided that for him.

Squatting down, he unzipped his backpack. From inside, he removed a set of folding panels. He set them out in the open to collect the energy from the muted sun. Solar cells were gold in this world, and that was another reason why he liked to leave right after a show. Some people would kill him for those solar panels. There wasn't much you couldn't do with them if you knew anything about wires and electricity.

He pulled the string of twinkle lights from around his chest and dropped them on the ground. These were followed by the clank of tent poles on dry dirt. He sat down in the dust and tried to piece them all together, but they seemed to have a mind of their own. In frustration, he pounded the dirt and muttered swears under his breath, but eventually, he was able to get the poles set up just right. He had two long poles, ten feet in length. In order to form a frame for his lights, he would plant one end of the pole into the ground, and then bend it and jam the other end in the ground, creating a V-like shape. He did the same with the other tent pole, and then, he strung the lights between the two v's, securing them in place with duct tape.

When his lights were set, he picked his sword up off the ground and jammed the tip into the loose, dry soil. The handle of his sword doubled as a removable microphone. A switch on the pommel of the handle turned the cross bar into a pair of lights that projected up at his face.

"You can never have enough lighting," the comedian said.

What if you're on fire? Is that too much lighting? Oddrey asked.

"Oh, Odd, you say the strangest things."

With everything in place, the comedian took the time to clean himself up a bit. Gingerly, he removed his dusty, but trusty, military jacket and placed it gently in the dirt behind his makeshift stage. He pushed his goggles up into his hair, and then by spitting on his hands, he cleaned his face. Not that he really needed it, but it never hurt. If a lady fancied you, that could lead to all sorts of sweet swag at the end of a show.

The shirt underneath his jacket was embarrassingly clean. Most people would look at it and assume it had been washed recently, but that's just how the comedian rolled. He never exposed his shirt except during performances. His fingerless gloves once again hid the pale flesh of his tan-lined hands.

He stood on a small berm of earth covered in fledgling weeds and grass that were barely holding on to life. Bouncing around and smashing the ground with his heel, he stomped on the grass until it was flat. Suddenly, his foot hit something hard, and he saw another of those tiny skulls hiding in the long grass. He reared his foot back and kicked it out of the way, and then he finished tamping down the stage.

When he completed his task, he looked up at the sky and smiled. Comedy was the only thing he had left, and while it paid the bills, namely, the bills of his body, it was something he would have done for free if given the chance. "Fuck yeah," he said as he admired his stage. He stood for a while, silently congratulating himself.

Yokel appeared, running across the grassy meadow.

"You pass 'em all out?" the comedian called.

"I got everyone. Even the merchant, and he likes me about as much as he likes you."

"Hey!" the comedian shouted.

Yokel stopped in his tracks, his words falling from his lips.

The comedian continued. "I do the jokes around here."

Yokel nodded bashfully.

The comedian pulled the stub of an old cigar from his pocket, lit it with a match, and puffed on it like his life depended on it. For the first time in weeks, he seemed at peace, as if the dust and stink of the wasteland were but images from an old forgotten movie and not reality. Bending down, he reached inside his military jacket and pulled out a roman candle. He held the firework's fuse up to his mouth and puffed and puffed on the cigar until the ancient fuse caught fire. It sparked fast, and the comedian held the roman candle aloft.

The fuse disappeared inside the cardboard cylinder, and nothing happened for a moment, and then a bright golden ball launched into the air, climbing and climbing until it exploded in a shower of sparks, the report echoing across the field between Shithole and the hungry forest. One after another, the roman candle fired off its bounty, illuminating the sky, reminding people of the good old days, the days when a country lauded as the most powerful in the world would celebrate its own bloody birth with excess and explosions. Or maybe it reminded them of the end of that country, reminded them of the lies it told, the deaths it was responsible for. Either way, it reminded them of something, something that wasn't the everyday struggle for survival, and those on the fence in Shithole, those who were fearful of a scam, of some sort of trick, they were able to put those doubts off to the side, shuffle them into the dark corners of their mind where memories of how the world used to be hid in the shadows. They could forget. For one glorious evening they could forget.

The residents of Shithole eyed each other, shrugged their shoulders, and packed up their blankets, their children, and some snacks, before venturing out the gates of the town, some of them for the first time in years. They came bearing torches, solar-powered lights on stakes that had been meant to light garden pathways in better times. They were worth a fortune, a mountain of beans, but today, the torches lit their path as the sun went down and the night came on, green and ugly. In addition to the pitiful residents of Shithole, the moon above struggled to fight its way through the ever-present cloud cover of a dying world to see the show.

The comedian watched them approach, and then he stepped off his makeshift stage and plugged in his lights. They glowed and twinkled, mini-stars to replace the ones obscured by nuclear haze and the last breaths of billions.

Yokel, unsure and awkward, stepped up onto the stage. Something inside him flipped, and though the words he said were ridiculous and his delivery mangled, the energy and passion with which he introduced the comedian more than made up for these flaws.

As he spoke, Yokel waved his hands in the air, giving it his all. "Step right up, ladies and gentlemen. One night only, the master of dis-laughter, the king of wisecracks, the server of snaps and sniggers. You know him, you hate him. The man that bested Beatums Sterling. The man that survived a night in the Flesh Paddlers' den and lived to tell the tale, the King of Cornhole, the funniest man since Fluffy walked the earth…" Yokel turned to the comedian and whispered, "I thought that up on my own." Then he turned back to the crowd as they found their seats. "Tonight only, a one-night stand at the end of the world. Ladies and gentleman and those in-between, it's my honor to present to you tonight, the comedian!"

The comedian had to hand it to the man; it was quite an introduction. As he watched the citizens of Shithole file in, he saw the anxiety and suspicion drain from their faces. Oh, they were still ready to bolt at the first sign of something amiss, but less-so thanks to Yokel's rousing introduction.

From the growing darkness behind the stage, the comedian heard a voice. He turned and saw a small, skinny man with curly hair standing in the shade among some scrub trees.

"You got this buuuuuuuuudddy!"

He knew that voice, knew it as his own god, knew it as his inspiration, his own personal deity.

"Thanks, Weaz." And with that, the comedian flicked his own switch. Bounding onto the stage, he smiled like a carnival barker, his arms spread wide.

Quickly, he scanned the crowd. They were all there, the merchant in his ridiculous get-up, his animatronic mask lit up like freaking Christmas. Mugs was there, a keg of beer sitting next to him in a rusted red wagon. To his right, Yokel sat, leaning forward, his legs crossed at the ankles, and a smile splitting his face almost in half. A family sat in the back: mannequin boy, a relatively normal-looking wife, a small sister pulling a child-size skull on a cooler that also doubled as a seat, and a dirty-looking fellow covered from head to toe in the remnants of shit. A tall man with dark eyes sat in a full rubber radiation suit, only his head exposed. In the back, a tottering woman, the healer, walked with the help of a tall man in a beat-up top hat. The pair was dressed to the wasteland nines in clothes that had once been appropriate for a high-society ball, but which were now so soiled and ripped they wouldn't be fit to donate to a homeless shelter.

In the front center, a woman sat, with dark eyes and a plump face. A skinny man with uncracked glasses, a rarity in the wasteland, sat next to her, and he could tell they were an item. Off to his left, Beatums himself sat, an eager smile on his face, the dusty points of his boots pointing up at the angry sky. Behind him sat a large man, his arms bulging with muscle, and covered in tattoos. His beard was long and his head hairless. In the failing light, it was hard to tell if the man was bald or had simply shaved his head. He didn't recognize the man, but his sixth sense tingled a bit as he made eye contact with him. The man looked like a murderous lumberjack, and the comedian marked him well.

In the very back, he saw a surprise. Ajax, she of the straight-laced, always serious demeanor, stood leaning against a wooden railing that had somehow survived the end of the world. Even in the coming twilight, he could see the green of her eyes burrowing into him, measuring and judging.

The only person not present was Sheriff Eldoon. He had probably stayed behind to guard Shithole. Maybe he wasn't all that stupid after all. Or maybe he was. Doing one street-smart thing didn't all of the sudden make someone a sage.

The comedian flipped the switch set into the cross-guard of his sword. Two bright LED lights set into the ends of the cross-guard flared to life, bathing the comedian's face in a bright, blue-white light. For those members of the audience who were old enough, they were reminded of days long past when adults would turn on flashlights, hold them under their chin, and try to scare the bejeezus out of ignorant children with spooky stories. The comedian twisted the grip of his sword and pulled the microphone handle free.

"Good evening ladies and gentleman. Step right up. Boy, have I got a show for you tonight! Sit right down. Grab a seat in the grass. It don't bite, though I've seen some that does, but that's a different story entirely."

160

Those that were still standing seemed comforted by the comedian's words, and they hunkered down in the grass. The grass itself was still, innocuous as if it too was paying attention to the comedian. The only person who didn't move or get comfortable was Ajax. She seemed fine leaning against her post.

The comedian smiled. "I know what you're thinking right now. You're thinking, is this a trap?"

Some people in the audience nodded.

"Well, no, it isn't, ladies and gentlemen. This is a privilege. You see, I'm a wanderer, a vagabond—like a drifter, I was born to walk alone." To punctuate his words, the comedian strutted back and forth across his stage, knowing that movement had a hypnotic effect upon the audience. The human mind loved to see movement, loved to see things happening. It was a poor comedian who stood stock-still on stage.

"For tonight, I just have one wish. I want you all to relax and have a good time. Let me take the burden from your shoulders for one evening."

The people in the crowd glanced at each other to see if everyone was buying what the comedian was selling.

A woman in the crowd, dark smudges of charcoal around her eyes in lieu of make-up, her face screwed up like a pensioner upon learning their coupon had expired, yelled in a faux cockney accent, "What do you get out of this, if your show is free?"

"Yeah," some in the audience echoed, their eyebrows raised in suspicion.

The comedian knew this was coming. It didn't matter where he did his show; no one believed that anything was free anymore, and well they shouldn't. "Some people are killers," he began in a soothing tone, charming them with his comforting voice. "Some are lovers. Some are scavengers. Some are slayers. Me? I'm none of those things. I'm just about the most worthless thing on the

161

planet—a comedian. The only skill I got is to make people laugh. But I make it work for me." The comedian flashed his teeth again, perfect white, lit by the glare of LED lights.

He waved his hand behind him and pulled a bandana from his back pocket, twisting it and making the cloth pop against the air. He held the bandana out to the audience, displaying the tie-dyed material, the colors faded and soft. Posturing like a magician, he turned the bandana back and forth in the air to show people he had nothing up his sleeve. Then he snapped the bandana in the air and let it drop like an autumn leaf upon the ground. Patting it straight with his gloved hands, he smoothed the wrinkles out of the cloth.

"Now, all I'm askin' is for you to give me a chance. Listen to me. Laugh with me. If, at the end of the night, you feel that I've benefited you at all, in any way, I ask for a donation of whatever you can afford. No donation is too big, but certainly no donation is too small either."

The crowd murmured a bit, muttering to each other. They still didn't quite believe him.

The comedian clapped his hands together, and some in the audience jumped like startled cats. "Deal?"

A few heads in the audience nodded. A few was enough.

"Good." The comedian turned to Yokel and spoke. "I forgot to ask you, what's the name of this town?" He knew full well what the name was. Hell, he'd been giggling internally about it since he first heard the name. But, a show was a show, and sometimes, to make it feel more natural, you had to get the audience involved.

Yokel looked around, equal parts embarrassed and honored at being singled out by the comedian. He sat up straight, his civic pride painted in brown paint upon his filthy shirt. "It's Shithole."

The comedian broke into fiendish laughter. He was good. It almost seemed real. "You're shitting me!"

162

The audience shook their heads to indicate that they were not, in fact, shitting the comedian.

"Well, hello, Shithole!" the comedian yelled, greeting the audience and breaking the ice. An audience liked to be acknowledged, even if it was only in reference to the town they lived in. That's a secret rock stars inherently knew from back when there were such things. Saying hello to a town did something to the audience, let them feel like they were part of the show. It warmed them somehow. "I can't believe you're still here. I've been to a lot of towns, but none ever called Shithole. Yeah, I been to a lot of towns around the wasteland. Been to Turnip. All they eat there is turnips. Not very original. I been to Taterburg, and all they eat there is potatoes. I just did a show over in Yamtown. You guys know Yamtown?"

Most members of the audience shook their heads.

"You know, you go across the quicksand, take a left at the killer worms. Yamtown! Fuckin' Yamtown! You know what they eat there?"

"Yams!" the audience yelled.

The comedian laughed as he continued. "Yams, fucking yams! I'm so fucking sick of yams I could puke. Yamburgers, yam milk, yam ham—which is just yam shaped like a ham. Reeeeaaaaal disappointing." The comedian took a deep breath, and then asked, "So uhhh... what do you guys eat in Shithole?"

As he scanned the audience, he caught sight of a man, a skinny balding man with sickly-looking skin the color of curdled milk. His mouth hung open in surprise at the comedian's question. A brown substance encircled the area around the man's mouth, and as they made eye contact, the sickly man stuck out his tongue and lightly licked at the brown stuff on his lips. Shocked, the comedian's eyes grew wide, and he quickly moved on to his next subject.

"Names. Fucking names. When did we all get so uncreative? It's like we don't even try with names anymore.

163

You know what I mean? Back when the world still worked and most people actually had ten fingers and ten toes, they would spend months trying to figure out a proper name for something. What should we call this razor for man pubes? They'd all get together, have a focus group, look up ideas on the internet, and in the end, they'd come up with some clever name like Bushwhacker or Manscaper, real clever shit like that. Now people just pull shit out of thin air. Now, I get it. It's the end of the world, most people are dead, cities are gone, but we need to stop it with these fucking names. You people are ridiculous! I was in this one camp, just a couple of months ago. Great place. Taco Town. You know what they eat there?"

He held out his mic to the audience, and the audience screamed, "Tacos!"

The comedian laughed. He had the audience in the palm of his hand. "Nope. Not a taco in sight. All they ate was burritos. But hey, they did have a chick with two mouths. Wasn't much to look at, but two mouths…" The comedian simulated sex by poking his index finger through a circle he made with his opposite hand. "…that's a lot of talking if you know what I mean."

Some of the men in the audience liked this joke, loved it in fact. One man let out a howl like a hyena, and he pumped his fist in the air. The women didn't like it so much, but hey, they couldn't all be winners.

"Anyway, in Taco Town, everyone's got a tough-ass name. I met a Gator, a Buzzsaw, a Terror." The comedian growled the names off, trying to make them sound tough as nails. "Terror's like thirteen-years-old and carries a slingshot around, weighs about a buck-ten and thinks he's king shit because he can knock beer cans off a fence. Nothing terrifying about him. It's like the world ended, and the first thing people said was, 'Hmmm, now that my parents are dead, and everyone else for the most part, I'm gonna go by the douchiest name possible.'" The comedian

164

paused and then scanned the audience. "You probably got someone like this in the audience right now. Am I right?"

A mocking murmur ran through the crowd. A man sitting next to the merchant elbowed him in the ribs. The comedian, his heart ringing with joy, pointed at the merchant, wondering why he had never inquired about the man's name. *Oh, yeah, I don't really give a shit.*

In a voice that sounded warm and welcoming, the comedian asked. "You sir, I see your friends have outed you. Can you tell me your name?"

The merchant, caught in the spotlight and with nowhere to run, looked left and right sheepishly. Then he mustered his pride, sat up straight, and said, "It's Murdertron."

"Oh, Jesus!" the comedian laughed. "That's a new one. Murdertron!"

The audience laughed along with him, and Murdertron wilted a bit.

"Murdertron. Half-robot, half-murder… does that get the ladies?" The comedian continued in his best impersonation of Arnold Schwarzenegger. "My name is Murdertron. Come with me if you want to live."

The people to Murdertron's left and right busted up laughing, and the merchant shoved them in anger.

The comedian, reveling in Murdertron's discomfort, forged ahead, loving every second of it. "What was your real name? You know, before everything fell apart."

The merchant shook his head, the wiry hair on his helmet shaking from side to side. His lips remained sealed.

The comedian could see that Murdertron was going to need a little more assurance to step willingly into his comedic trap. "Oh, come on, man. We gotta know! I mean, there's no shame here. It's the end of the world, man. You wanna talk embarrassment? The other day, I was walking down the street, and I started to feel all sexy like. You know what I mean? Like that feeling you get when all of a sudden, you're like very aware of something residing in this area right here." The comedian waved his hand over his crotch area, and he saw some faces nod knowingly in the audience, grunting like cavemen.

"I'm walking down the street, and I'm all, 'Fuck it.' Let's do this. What the hell? Kill two birds with one stone. Get to town and GET TO TOWN! So I whip out Big Bird and start giving him a choking he's never gonna forget." On his makeshift stage, the comedian throws back his head and mimics walking and pleasuring himself.

"For those who have ever tried walkin' and caulkin', let me just say it takes a hell of a lot of concentration. I mean, you gotta make sure you're moving, but you still gotta be paying attention. You don't want to trip and fall on your engorged member. That could lead to disaster. There's not a lot of doctors left out there. Last doctor I found in my journeys was a proctologist. I get it, you're a real doctor, but no one feels like you're a real doctor. Everyone just kind of thinks you're some sort of super-smart pervert who figured out a way to legally put things into people's asses to get your kicks. Am I wrong or am I wrong?"

The comedian turned to the audience, and they all mumbled their assent, just like he knew they would.

"So I'm doing my shuffle, the jerk shuffle if you will, and I'm into it, man." The comedian leaned back, aiming his face up at the night sky above. He squeezed his eyes shut, bit his lower lip, and continued his sexual pantomime. "I'm thinking of like the sexiest thing I've ever seen. His name—er—her name was Sam. Used to clean the pool in my neighbor's backyard. I'd watch her in her little shorts… just dipping out leaves." Stroke. "Fast Times at Ridgemont style. So hot." Stroke. "I close my eyes for a second. It's just me, my hand, and Sam." Stroke. "Suddenly, I hear a sound." The comedian stopped, his hand in mid-stroke. "I open my eyes, and I'm standing there, face to face with some other dude, and I'm like

'Whoa!' I pause and this dude's just staring at me with these drippy bugeyes. He doesn't say anything. Then, I just sort of test it out..."

The comedian, with the audience hanging on his every word, mimed a slow-stroke to his implied gear. "I give it a slow one. The guy does nothing. So I'm like this..."

This time, the comedian does a couple of fast strokes.

"The guy still stands there. So I'm like alright, I'm just gonna finish this off—make a trade. Maybe this guy has some goldfish crackers or some shit. I'd kill a motherfucker for some goldfish crackers."

The audience nodded in agreement. Goldfish crackers were literally as good as gold these days.

"So I start going to town. All the romance is gone." The comedian's hand moved faster than the eye could see. "It's business time. I'm going so fast, I look like E. Honda in Street Fighter 2."

The comedian paused for laughter, but none was forthcoming. The crowd was dead quiet and staring at him like he was some sort of freak.

He shrugged and continued. "No? No nerds in the audience? That's ok. I'll adjust. So there I am, going to town, out of politeness, and then this guy, he reaches down to *his* crotch and starts to unzip *his* pants, and I'm all, 'Whoa! Whoa! Whoa! What are you doin', pal?'"

The comedian paused and scanned the audience, a look of disbelief on his face as he continued. "The guy looks at me and says in this real dry voice, like he hadn't had a drink of water since the Internet was a thing, and he says, 'It's all good in the poxyclypse.' Then the guy starts getting this look in his eye... and I'm like oh, shit. I'm in trouble."

The comedian, still stroking air, looked around the audience with fear on his face. "The guy pulls out his stuff, and I can't help but look, cuz secretly I'm hoping it's microscopic because then I'd know a hundred-percent that I don't have the smallest dick in the apocalypse. That's important to a man. A man walks taller when he knows that he's lengthier than at least one person out there. So he whips it out, and I'm disappointed." On stage, the comedian deflated, his head drooping to his chest. "Not only am I not bigger than this guy, but he's basically working a mannequin arm down there, and I can tell he wants to do more than just polish the old banister. This dude wants to get biblical."

The comedian paused for dramatic effect. He hiked his pants up and looked off into the distance. "Long story short, the goldfish were delicious. You guys got a proctologist around here?"

The crowd laughed at this last part, and the comedian silently congratulated himself on his timing. "See, Murdertron? Ain't no thing about being embarrassed. I just told a story about butt stuff in exchange for goldfish, and you can't tell us what your real name is?"

Murdertron shook his head.

"Come on. Be a pal," the comedian prodded. "Come on, Murd. You can do it."

Murdertron looked around sheepishly. He pulled his helmet off, and the comedian was once again struck by how soft the man's face looked. Maybe that was the reason he wore the helmet in the first place. Sometimes looking tough was a better deterrent than actually being tough.

In a faint, almost embarrassingly quiet voice, Murdertron began, "It was…"

"Go on," the comedian prodded when he stalled.

"It was Todd."

At this revelation, the comedian couldn't help himself, and he burst into a giant guffaw of laughter. The audience joined in, echoing the comedian's chortles.

The comedian, knowing that maybe he had gone too far with his response, offered an olive branch to Murdertron... sort of. "Jesus, I'm sorry dude. Todd—life must have been a nightmare for you."

Tears streamed from the merchant's eyes.

"I mean. I'm a comedian, but there's some things you just don't joke about. Todd. Did your parents not want a kid? Todd's like a gerbil's name. Todd's like when you take an epic dump, and it's so brown and gnarly, you just have to give it a name. Todd is what you call that dump. Yep, no doubt about it." The comedian paused to let his words sink in. "But here's where you messed up, Todd. You don't go from Todd to Murdertron. Just like you don't go from learning to walk to running a marathon. You don't go from fingerbanging Oozy Lucy on the slagfarm to rocking out in a no-holes-barred orgy. Baby steps, Todd."

The comedian paused then, both to catch his breath and to think for a moment. The stage was like a whirlwind, and a good comedian knew when to stop, take a moment and let the possibilities swirl in their mind. An idea came to him, and he ran with it.

"No, I think badass names have to be earned in increments. We should all have levels like we're in an old video game. Say what you will about video games, but they had the world right. Murdertron should be like your reward for reaching the highest level. You start out a Todd. Then, let's say you kill off a raider or something. Then you can upgrade your name, start calling yourself something like..." The comedian's fingers twitched in the air as he searched for a name that would be a slight upgrade to Todd. "...Betty!"

From the back of the audience, an angry voice called out, interrupting the comedian's flow. "And what's wrong with the name Betty?" The comedian noticed Ajax standing against the fence post. Her cloak was thrown backwards, and her hand rested upon the handle of her mace, the promise of violence reflecting off the steel. He panicked then, thrown off his game.

"Uhh... nothing! Betty's a great name. Kill a raider, you get to be a Betty. Everyone knows you're a raider-killer. On top of that, at this point, Betty is actually a badass name because everyone else's name is so ridiculously over-the-top."

He watched as Ajax mulled over his explanation. The anger melted from her face, and she let her cloak fall back into place. She nodded at the comedian, and relieved, he continued the show.

"So anyway, let's say Betty's not a badass enough name for you." He nodded apologetically to Ajax in the back, but all she did was glare at him with those green eyes. "You want something that pops, something that sings. Well, just drag your ass to a fallout shelter and slay ten zombies. Boom! You're now Dwayne! Murdertron... shit, you should basically have to be sitting on a pile of your enemies' skulls before you could ever call yourself Murdertron. You should have to walk into a fortified place like the Fortress of Good, slay the entire town in hand-to-hand combat, and then take a big dump right in the middle of town before you can call yourself Murdertron!"

A series of *yeahs* went up from the crowd, and though he wasn't bothered by crushing the spirit of Murdertron, he decided to offer him another olive branch... kind of. "Well, let's get Todd a new name. I can't call you Murdertron because you're not sitting on a pile of skulls. What's your most badass accomplishment, Todd?"

The merchant, his helmet back on his head to hide the remains of his tears, sat up proudly. "I killed a thief last year!"

"There you go. Killed a thief. That's something."

The woman with the angry face called out, interrupting the comedian's flow. "Boooooo! He was a one-armed lepper from the wastes!"

170

The comedian laughed slightly as he saw Murdertron slump in the crowd. "Is that true, Todd?"

"He knew kung fu," the merchant said in defense.

The comedian laughed again, secretly smiling about Murdertron, his own personal comedy gold mine. If there was a god above, he was certainly smiling down on him that evening. "Let me get this straight. Your greatest accomplishment is that you killed a one-armed scabby man?"

Murdertron whined, "He was big though!"

"Great. Got it," the comedian said dismissively. "Tall, one-armed scabby man. Let me put that into my wasteland tough-guy name generator."

The comedian bent over as if he was looking into a computer screen. He mimed typing on a keyboard, producing all sorts of beeps and boops with his mouth, and then he stood up with a smile on his face. "Aha! I got it! Your name is… Cripple Killer!"

The crowd laughed at the merchant's new name.

The comedian, a large grin on his face, said, "It's not P.C., so you know it's tough."

Yokel, off to the comedian's right, howled with laughter. In between breaths he yelled mockingly and pointed. "Cripple Killer!" Then he giggled like a goon, rocking back on the seat of his dusty jeans and slapping his thighs.

The comedian reveled in the uproar. Was it fair to destroy the merchant in the process? He didn't know, or maybe he didn't care, or maybe the thought never even crossed his mind.

From there, the comedian flowed, weaving a spell like a magician. In his mind, he imagined an invisible net, comprised of words and jokes. At the beginning of the night, it started off high in the air, sparkling in a way only he could see. With each chortle, each laugh, the threads of the net grew thicker, shinier until they twinkled like stars.

171

He shared of himself upon the stage, baring his soul, his experiences, the nightmares, the good and the bad, and through it all, he laced his particular brand of humor, filthy but sincere. The crowd fell into it, and over the course of the night, the net descended upon them, weighed down by goodwill until he was theirs and they were his. Like lovers, they reveled in each other's company.

After a bit about orange-skinned people in a blast zone around what had once been the city of Memphis, the comedian licked his lips and fell into a silent daze. Yokel, the jokes sailing over his head with a frequency that left him feeling dumb, scratched at his greasy hair. Feeling slightly awkward, Beatums produced a tiny cough and with this, the comedian snapped out of his memories.

"So what's with these guys I've seen around lately? I guess a lot of things haven't changed. Still got 'the law.' Anyone had their teeth kicked in for takin' a second yam, or in your case, a log?" The comedian pointed at the man with the shit be-ringed mouth, and the man smiled like a doof in response.

"You know these guys? The Chicken Kickers? You seen these fucks? They walk around in their white tabards. Ooh, don't make the mistake of calling it a shirt. They get all bent out of shape." The comedian stood up straight and spoke in an erudite voice, 'It's a tabard, not a shirt.' Psshh. Have you ever seen a more uptight group of people in your life? Fuck, I thought cops were bad before the bombs. Now we got these Chicken Kickers walking around laying beatings on people they think are *bad*. Like, who the hell are you, in your stupid shirts and your chainmail, to come along and tell us what's bad? You're telling me that with all the shit we have to worry about, the radioactivity, the mutant monsters, the red hats, the zombies, the guy that always wants to shake your hand, now we've got these guys on our ass? Every time I waste a raider, I gotta look over my shoulder and make sure one of these tabarded freaks isn't standing there waiting to bash my head in with a freaking mace. A mace! A fucking metal ball on the end of a stick!"

"Beyooooo! They're awful," the angry-faced woman in the audience yelled.

Shocked by the glorious accent of the woman, the comedian did a double-take. "I see you got that wasteland accent there. I like it. World goes to shit, and everyone starts sounding like a cockney Michael Caine. 'Oh, ello guvna, fancy a mace to the skull?' But yeah, they are awful."

The comedian was worked up now, and his true rage showed through. He bent over and looked the audience members in the eyes. "It's the fucking wasteland! Who the hell are you to tell me I can't waste a raider, shove a stick up his ass, and leave him rotting on the side of I-5? He stole my Beefaroni! You know how rare it is to find Beefaroni these days? I don't like it. I don't like it one bit. These Chicken Kickers. You know what they call criminals?"

"What?" some member of the audience asked.

"Chickens! 'Here now, chicken, did you just tell a lie? I shall kick you in the name of justice.' No fun these guys. I mean, the only good thing about these people is they pretty much have to catch you in the act. Yeah, they gotta see you sticking that stick in that dead raider's butt because we don't have any way for them to find chickens. There's no fingerprints, no DNA. You wanna spray your load on that raider corpse, go ahead. No one's matching up chromosomes anymore."

The comedian shook his head. It was hard to believe what the world was coming to these days. "I hear all the Chicken Kickers come from a town five raider checkpoints to the south. Yeah, they made a village out there, out of like a Tyson's chicken factory. I was always a Purdue man myself. They call it The Coop. Apparently, they have some sort of god they worship, some sort of being they believe is the chosen one."

The comedian ran a hand thoughtfully through his beard. "Out on the road, I met an old woman who was missing all her teeth… an eye, a foot, she was missing a lot of things. I traded her half a harmonica for a spoonful of beans, and I had dinner there while she gummed that harmonica. She says that all the Chicken Kickers worship Betty White's character in the Golden Girls."

The comedian locked eyes with Ajax, but she didn't react. She stared right back at him, cold and unshaken. "Apparently, they have a TV set up down there, and all they have to play on it is a collection of Golden Girls and Marvel movies. Imagine how twisted your world-view would be if all you had to watch was Golden Girls and Marvel movies? You'd have like no sense of humor, and you'd try to solve all your problems with violence. Oh, did you tell a lie? Let me beat the ever-loving shit out of you. Chicken Kickers… they're the chickens, afraid of letting the world run its course."

He paused then and looked around the audience. He had them all in his pocket. "Chicken Kickers, like it's not enough to have the zombies, the human-sized bats, all those S and M raiders with their buttcheeks flapping in the wind. Now we gotta have these goodie-goodies looking over our shoulder making sure you're not putting your thumb on the scale when you trade a bullet for a cupful of carrot shavings. Come on! We all know about the thumb! We don't need you changing things. Haven't we had enough change as it is? We just got used to it, and they're gonna come along and try and fix things to what they were? No thanks. I don't need some tabarded asshole telling me I'm walking too fast through a residential neighborhood."

The comedian had infuriated himself, and he lashed out on stage. "Chicken Kicker! I'll kick you!" He kicked out at the air and made a fairly good imitation of a squawking chicken.

"You ask me, they're the chickens. Afraid of a little lie here and there. That's just a mole, baby. It's always been down there… Frankly, I'm surprised you didn't notice it. Don't you love me?"

The audience laughed at this. Even Murdertron, his tears now dried to his cheeks, was able to chuckle a bit.

"God, could you imagine if we all actually told the truth a hundred-percent of the time? There'd be no fun in this world. Part of surviving a raider attack is the tension. It wouldn't be much fun if one of these shoulder-pad-wearing fucks came up to your campfire at night. You're sitting there, slowly chewing a Vienna sausage you found in a glove box of a broken-down Toyota Tercel."

He mimicked chewing daintily on a Vienna sausage, staring off into the cloudy sky.

"That's how we eat now. Like fucking gerbils. I once found a granola bar and ate it grain by grain just to make it last. Took me all night… and then this guy stumbles out of the woods. And they always look surprised. Always. Like, 'Oh, fancy finding another living soul out here.' What? You're blind and have no sense of smell? You couldn't see the fire and smell the smoke? He's wearing a hockey helmet, some shoulder pads, fingerless gloves. He has a mullet and assless chaps. 'Can I share your fire?' they always ask, like you were born after the vampiric rift opened in Yellowstone. They sit down, and they're all shady, trying to scope out if you're worth the trouble of robbing out of the corner of their eyes. Oh, the tension! It's so great! Your heart starts beating so fast you can hear it in your ears, like you just stepped into a bomb crater and absorbed a million rads all at once. What if I just asked, 'Are you gonna try and kill me?' If he can't lie, he's just gonna be like, 'Well, yeah. Duh.' No fun at all. That's like going up to someone and asking them if they wanna have sex? They say yes. One of you gets it in there, and it's all over. Where's the fun in that? I mean that guy's probably used to it...

The comedian pointed at Yokel, who smiled and laughed like a goof, looking self-consciously at the other villagers around him.

"...but the rest of us, we wanna be romanced a little before you try and kill us. I want you to pretend like you're just some harmless dude in shoulder pads with a bit of human flesh stuck between your teeth. That's how you can tell, you know. These raiders, they never floss. Human is stringy from what I've heard."

Sighing deeply, the comedian looked to the sky once more, clearly disappointed with himself. "You know, I promised I wasn't going to keep doing this. Listen, let's all just stop pretending. None of us would be here if we hadn't eaten a little human every now and then. Can we all agree that yeah, sometimes we eat other people? It's ok. Better than possum skewers, that's for damn sure."

The audience nodded, and the man in the radiation gear muttered an audible, "Damn right."

"Aha! I got you fuckers! Cannibal freaks. I knew it! Every last one of you. So who is it, huh? Who's the weirdo that always eats the genitals? You got a whole roasted body for the camp to eat, and there's always that one guy that goes for the bits. Innie, outie, it don't matter. He wants to eat it."

The audience points to Murdertron.

"Cripple Killer? Cripple Killer's the freak? Try something different next time, man. Go for a nice thigh cut, or a rump steak. You gotta live a little."

He shook his head at Murdertron, and the merchant's head drooped a little bit.

"That's what it's all about, right? Living a little? I mean, when the world hands you shit, you dig a little hole, and name your town after it. Am I right?" He looked over

176

the crowd, and he could see them mulling over his words. When they were ready, he swiped a hand across his mouth to remove the dried spittle from his lips. Then he said, "You know what I miss?"

The crowd screamed into the comedian's proffered mic. "What?"

"I miss weekends. I mean, we don't get weekends anymore. Every day is the same in the apocalypse. Survive a raider attack, eat some dirt, absorb more rads, search through cupboards other people have searched through a hundred times already… think about killing yourself. It all blends together. Like, no one even knows what day it is anymore. Shit, I'm not even sure what year it is. All the calendars are done now. Like, is it Tuesday? Should we all be pissed off and going to bed at eight o'clock to wake up for another day of digging in the dirt and trying not to get killed by a mutant gopher that pops up out of the ground? Is it Friday? Am I supposed to be chugging down cans of beer and trying to get a little action from the crone in the woods who makes her living doing curses on the side?

"I had a beer a few weeks ago in this town, about thirty crucified corpses down the road. It's called Brewtown, of course. So I pass over a roll of copper wire, and I get myself a beer. I sit at the table. There's some guy on a kazoo playing Macklemore songs. I sit in the corner, so they can't shank me and steal all my shit, and I take a sip of the beer. It's warm; it tastes like beer. I drank it down, and I felt nothing. Where's the joy?

"And then it hit me, beer is only good after you've worked all week. You wanna know what I did that whole week? I sat in an abandoned post office reading the mail and eating a bag of jerky that only made me shit for two days straight. So, when I strolled into that town looking to trade, I hadn't earned it.

"A beer, bubbly, effervescent, is only good if you've earned it. If you haven't earned it, it just makes you feel

177

like a loser. I'm halfway through it, and I'm all, 'What am I doing with my life?' I should be out looking for scrap or bottlecaps or something. I should be out setting traps for raiders in the woods or smashing in zombie heads, you know, actual productive member of society type shit."

The comedian fell silent as he paced back and forth on stage, his head down, his mind playing with his own thoughts. Eventually, he looked up and smiled at the audience.

"But hey, I'm happy to report that the second beer tastes better. I traded them half a bar of used Irish Spring I found in a collapsed farmhouse and a rubber that might still be good for another use, and all that shit went away, and it was the best damn beer that I'd ever had. Until the third one and the one after that.

"So I guess what I'm trying to say is, even though things might not be going your way, and you start to have those self-doubts—you start to feel like you're not really a Murdertron, you're more of a Todd, or you start to feel like maybe no one is buying your wasteland accent, or you start to feel like maybe you want to be one of those stupid, worthless Chicken Kickers, just remember to keep doing what you're doing.

"Hey, it's what I do, and look at me. I'm pretty happy." The comedian smiled enthusiastically. "And with that, I'm gonna get up out of here. Have a good night, and I hope all of the shit you make in Shithole is the best quality shit one can find. This really is the best Shithole I've ever been to."

With that, the comedian bowed, low and deep. He would have described it as a Shakespearian bow. Members of the audience clapped politely, and the buzz of quiet conversation filled the meadow in front of town.

He turned his back to the audience then, eager not to spook off his prey. Wastelanders were much the same across the country. Many of them had lost the ways of

178

common decency, but for some, they still believed in paying their way. It seemed like there were less and less as the years dragged on, but someone, seeing his empty bandana, would pony up some form of currency.

In order to hasten their kindness, he busied himself with the disassembly of his stage. He unplugged the Christmas lights from the solar panels., saving their charge for another day.

Behind him, he heard the furtive footsteps of his patrons, and he managed to keep busy, lest he spook them off. When the footsteps all faded away through the tall grass, the comedian stood in a dark meadow, alone with only the green sky above and the forgotten face of the moon glowing behind the clouds to keep him company. He wadded up his bandana and shoved it in his backpack, eager to be away from Shithole. He had much ground to gain.

Chapter 14: Cold, Pink Meat and The After-Party

The comedian sat upon hard ground, ancient dried mud, dark and brown. A small fire of dried logs burned fragrantly, illuminating the immediate area around him. Though all he wanted to do was sleep, he had to see what the villagers at Shithole had given him.

His massive sword, now one piece again, sat behind him as he leaned against an ancient tree trunk. He had only taken the wood the forest had given him, refusing to pull anything from the trees that they were not ready to give up. The trees themselves seemed to shrink away from the fire.

I hope you got a doll body, Oddrey said, a tiny bit of hope in her voice.

"Yeah, we'll see." He reached into his backpack to examine his miniscule haul. He knew it wouldn't be much; it never was. The bandana weighed almost nothing when he picked it up. Placing the balled-up bandana on his lap, he unfolded its edges. "Ah, let's see what we got here."

He picked up the first item and held it up to the firelight. A small, shiny screw sparkled in the light from the fire. The comedian shook his head, it wasn't nothing, but it wasn't something either. He was sure he could find some use for it.

He plucked another item from the bandana. It was soft and tubular in his hand. As he held it out to the fire, his stomach dropped at its pink hue. Was this cold meat one of Murdertron's tasty bits taken from a human corpse? Still unsure of the clammy meat in his hand, he held it up to his nose. *Ah, a half-eaten Vienna sausage.* He smiled and took a mini-bite, chewing ever so slowly and savoring the salty goodness in his mouth. A yellow balloon, in fairly good shape, and a filthy sock with a hole in the toe rounded out his haul. Sadly, he'd had worse.

The comedian set the other items on the ground and picked up the partially eaten Vienna sausage. He took the smallest nibble from the tip, and then tried to play his customary, post-performance game of guessing who had given him what.

He wasn't playing long before he heard a sound in the woods that pricked up his ears. He eased his knife in its sheathe where it was buckled to his right thigh. That rustling in the woods sounded too clumsy to be an animal, and if it wasn't an animal... well, it could be lots of things, but it was almost always a—

The raider stepped out of the trees, stumbling in the darkness. The comedian recognized the man, knew his face, though not his name. He recognized his bald head from the show. His arms were tatted, and weapons and buckles and straps seemed to sprout from his body. His beard, burly and tangled, glowed in the light of the fire.

"Oh, I didn't know anyone was out here. Do you mind if I share your fire?" he asked in a gentle voice.

The comedian nodded. "Sure, as long as you're not going to kill me."

In a mocking voice that rang of disingenuousness, the raider said, "Oh, no. I'm just a simple traveler."

As the man smiled at him, the comedian saw the tell-tale flecks of pink-gray meat in his teeth. Smiling, the funnyman leaned back against the tree stump. His shoulders rocked up and down as small waves of silent laughter ran through his body. He took another rabbit-bite of the Vienna sausage, enjoying the electric tension that ran through his muscles.

Chapter 15: Ajax Burned the Meat

Blood dripped from the raider's sliced throat, dribbling down an ancient Led Zeppelin T-Shirt. Ajax didn't know what a Led Zeppelin was, and she didn't know what the picture on the shirt was either. It looked like some sort of giant shape burning in the sky. Maybe the shape was a zeppelin? If so, maybe it was made out of lead.

She stood up and examined the raider corpse once again. The dead man had his arms pulled back and wrapped around a tree trunk. On the backside of the tree trunk, his wrists had been bound together with a belt.

The raider's possessions, anything of value, had been taken. All that was left were his clothes, ancient and ripe.

Studying the raider's face for the tenth time, she began putting the pieces of the crime scene together. His mouth was drawn back in a terrifying grin, a gray tongue resting like a slug in his open mouth. A bungee cord wrapped around the tree, its ends fish-hooked through the raider's cheeks to pull the raider's mouth into a macabre smile. Dried streams of blood ran from the puncture wounds.

"I'm sorry. I should have followed him after the show." But she had needed to say goodbye to Comet and Silver. They were heading back to The Coop.

Ajax bent down and unbound the raider. He might have been a murderer, and judging by the flesh between his teeth, a cannibal, but he didn't deserve to have his corpse treated in this manner, staged like an amused audience member.

The comedian was sick. She had heard tell of mysterious murders like this in the past, heard whispers of a dark funnyman who traveled the wastes, making his living off weak humor. Though she didn't find him

182

particularly funny, he was the only comedian she had ever seen. Everywhere he went, chaos seemed to follow. Even now, the town of Shithole was tearing itself apart. Beatums had lit out in the morning, as had Sheriff Eldoon. No one could find the merchant or Yokel, and even Mugs was talking about closing up shop. Shithole would be a ghost town in no time at all. The comedian had to be stopped.

Ajax struggled to pull the bungee cord from the raider's mouth, and eventually, in her effort to remove it, the flesh of his cheeks ripped. She could have cut the cord, but a bungee cord was too valuable an item to destroy for the sake of a raider. Still, she apologized to the corpse as she dragged him to the pyre she had built.

She waited for the fire to take hold, and when she was sure the flames would cleanse his corpse, she turned her eyes east. In the dirt, she spied the comedian's trail, leisurely, unconcerned. She followed, conserving her energy, for at the end of her journey, there would be a reckoning. The comedian needed to be stopped, and she was the only one who cared to do it.

A Word From Jacy

Thank you for reading *One Night Stand at the End of the World*! If you've made it this far, I'm guessing you enjoyed the ride. Please leave a review! As an indie author, the only marketing I receive is from fellow readers like you!

If you enjoyed One Night Stand at the End of the World, check out the sequel, One Night Stand in the Wastes! And then check out the threequel, One Night Stand in Ike! The comedian's journey continues! Watch as he encounters strange characters, strange lands, and his own strange mind. The comedian's journey will continue. Right now, I'm not sure how many books will be in the series, but if it goes on forever, I wouldn't mind, as I have so much fun writing them!

Click the link below to check out One Night Stand in the Wastes!

Available on amazon!

Get Free Stuff from Jacy Morris

Building a relationship with my readers is super important to me. Please join my newsletter for information on new books and deals plus all this free content:

1. A free copy of This Rotten World: Part One.

2. A free copy of The Lady That Stayed, a horror novella inspired by real life.

3. A free copy of The Pied Piper of Hamelin, a twisted fairy tale like nothing you've ever seen before.

You can get your content for free, by signing up at:
https://landingpage.jacymorris.com/home-copy-1

Also By Jacy Morris

In the One Night Stand Series

One Night Stand at the End of the World

The world is gone, and it's not coming back. The rules have changed, but one man refuses to lay down and die. A comedian, shattered and broken, wanders the wasteland on a quest that only he knows and understands. Zombies, raiders, talking doll heads, shady merchants and unbeatable gamblers all stand in the way of The Comedian's success, but through the power of comedy, he will find a way.

Available on amazon!

One Night Stand in the Wastes

Book two in the One Night Stand series. With his sights set on a mysterious place named Ike, the comedian journeys across a shattered and broken wasteland, confronting demons both inner and outer. Behind him, justice dogs his footsteps in the form of Ajax, a ruthless arbiter of order who is hellbent on ending the comedian's chaotic ways. Killer squirrels, mutated humans, and raiders galore await the comedian in the blasted lands.

Available on amazon!

One Night Stand in Ike

Book three in the One Night Stand series. After journeying across the wastes, the comedian and his companion finally make their way to the town of Ike. There they find a twisted world based upon the rules of corporate society. In order for the comedian to complete his quest, the pair of survivors must play by the rules of Ike's regional manager… or they could, you know, kill everyone. We'll see.

Available on amazon!

In the This Rotten World Series

This Rotten World

A sickness runs rampant through the world. In Portland, Oregon it is no different. As the night takes hold, eight men and women bear witness to the horror of a zombie outbreak. This Rotten World is the zombie novel that horror fans have been waiting for. Where other zombie works skip over the best part of a zombie outbreak, This Rotten World revels in it the downfall of humanity, dragging you through the beginnings of society's death, kicking and screaming.

Available on amazon!

This Rotten World: Let It Burn

It didn't take long for Portland, Oregon to fall. Amid a decaying and crumbling city, a group of survivors hides amid the smoke and the fire. They need to get out of the city... which is easier said than done with thousands of zombies blocking the path. Witness the terrifying flight of these survivors as they leave the city behind and Let It Burn.

Available on amazon!

This Rotten World: No More Heroes

With the smoking ruins of Portland behind them, our survivors find that they have a new enemy to contend with... other survivors. With the dead hounding them at every step and humanity struggling to hold onto its civility, the survivors face their greatest challenge yet. At the end of this battle, there will be No More Heroes.

Available on amazon!

This Rotten World: Winter of Blood

Winter falls hard on Oregon, burying the world under snow and ice. One group of survivors, stuck in a tomb of their own creation, fights to survive, while another group treks across the snowbound countryside, leaving a trail of bloody footprints in their wake... and an army of the undead. The Pacific Ocean calls. Safety calls. But as Mother Nature rakes her frozen claws across the land, the coast could hardly seem further away. Will our survivors make it through this Winter of Blood, or will they be buried by an avalanche of the dead? Find out in the thrilling 4th installment of This Rotten World... This Rotten World: Winter of Blood.

Available on amazon!

This Rotten World: Choking on the Ashes

As our survivors near the coast, the road takes its toll. Falling apart physically and emotionally, they are drawn to the siren call of the beach. Seaside awaits them, a town demolished by a tsunami and crawling with the reanimated. With infants in tow, the survivors must band together to fight for a new home. All that stands between them and the future is an army of the dead. Will they succeed, or will they find themselves Choking on the Ashes?

Available on amazon!

This Rotten World: Rally and Rot

Introducing an entirely new cast of characters, Rally and Rot continues This Rotten World's tradition of zombie excellence. Every summer, Monktree, Wyoming holds a biker rally, an underground event policed by the bikers themselves. When a tragic accident kicks off the zombie apocalypse, the survivors must band together to make it out of town.

Available on amazon!

In the Enemies of Our Ancestors Series

The Enemies of Our Ancestors

In the mountains of the Southwest, in the time before the continents were known, the future of the entire world rested upon the shoulders of a boy prophet whose abduction would threaten to break the world. As a youth, Kochen witnessed the death of his father at the hands of a gruesome spirit that stalked his village's farmlands. From that moment forth, he became a ward of the priests of the village in the cliffs. As he grew, he would begin to experience horrific visions, gifts from the spirits, that all of the other priests dismissed. When the ancient enemies of the Cliff People raid the village and steal Kochen away, they set in motion world-changing events, which threaten to break the shackles that bind the spirits to the earth. A group of hunters are sent to bring Kochen back to his rightful place. As Kochen's power grows, so too does the power of the spirits, and with the help of an ancient seer and his hunter allies, he seeks to restore balance to the world as it falls into brutal madness.

Available on amazon!

The Enemies of Our Ancestors: The Cult of the Skull

With the world balanced after the tragedies of the year before, two tribes attempt to come together and form a whole. But as an ancient foe from the past reappears and a new threat from the south snakes its way to them, the Stick People and the Cliff People must do more than put their differences aside... they must come together to survive. As fantastic as it is violent, The Cult of the Skull picks up right where The Enemies of Our Ancestors left off.

Available on amazon!

The Enemies of Our Ancestors: Broken Spirits

Time has passed. The children of the tribes have grown. Peace has reigned as three tribes have tried to learn to live together. But now, an old terror rears its head. Together, the three tribes will have to learn to fight as one. The thrilling conclusion to The Enemies of Our Ancestors series.

Available on amazon!

Standalone Novels

The Abbey

In the desolate mountains of Scotland, there is an abbey that time has forgotten. Its buildings have crumbled, and the monks that once lived there, guarding the abbey's secret, are long dead. When the journal of a crazed monk is discovered, so is the secret of Inchorgrath Abbey. There are tunnels underneath the abbey and in them resides a secret long forgotten. Together with a group of mercenaries, her would-be boyfriend, and her cutthroat professor, Lasha Arkeketa will travel across the world to uncover the secret of The Abbey.

Available on amazon!

The Drop

How many hearts can a song touch? How many ears can it reach? How many people can it kill? When popular boy band Whoa-Town releases their latest album, no one thinks anything of it. They certainly don't think that the world will be changed forever. After an apocalyptic disease sweeps the world, it becomes clear that the music of this seemingly innocuous boy band had something to do with it, but how? Katherine Maddox, her life irrevocably changed by a disease dubbed The Drop, sets out to find out how and why, to prevent something like The Drop from ever happening again.

Available on amazon!

The Pied Piper of Hamelin

A sickness has come to the village of Hamelin. Born on the backs of rats, a plague begins to spread. As the town rips itself apart, a stranger appears to offer them salvation. But when the citizens of the town fail to hold up their end of the bargain, the stranger returns and exacts a toll that is still spoken of to this day. That toll? The town's entire population of children. This is the legend of the Pied Piper. It is no fairy tale. It is a nightmare. Are you prepared to hear his song?

Available on amazon!

Killing the Cult

At any one time, there are 4,000 cults operating within the United States. In Logansport, Indiana, one cult is growing. When The Benevolent recruit Matt Rust's estranged daughter, he journeys to their compound to free her, one way or another. Unfortunately, for Matt Rust, his checkered past threatens to derail his rescue mission. When word gets out that Rust has reemerged after spending the last decade in the witness protection program, drug tzar Emilio Cartagena sends his best men after Rust. Will he be able to save his daughter before Cartagena's men arrive? Find out as Matt Rust tries Killing the Cult.

Available on amazon!

The Lady That Stayed

Land has a price. It's always been that way. When J.S. Stensrud and his wife Dotty buy a piece of land on the Oregon coast known as the Spit, they come to know that price. As Stensrud tries to build a legacy on his island amid the background of the Great Depression, he is visited by a Native American woman who helps him learn the bloody price of land in the most painful way possible.

Available on amazon!

The Taxidermied Man

Bud got stuffed, and now he has a front row seat to the downfall of man.

Suffering from early-onset dementia due to alcoholism, Bud wants nothing more than to be there for his wife forever—so he has his body stuffed. Unfortunately, his wife is not at all pleased, and after she dies, Bud is sold off to the highest bidder only to be used as a sex toy, a sports trophy, and finally a God. As his imprisoned mind unravels, Bud witnesses the collapse of humanity through static eyes and an unchanging body.

Available on amazon!

An Unorthodox Cure

Cancer will touch all of our lives at one point or another. It may affect someone you know, someone you respect, or even someone you love. In the case of the Cutters, it has systematically invaded every cell of their daughter's body. When the doctors admit there is nothing they can do, the Cutters bring their daughter home and prepare to wait for the inevitable. Just as they accept defeat, a mysterious doctor appears at their door, offering a miraculous cure and kindling hope in their hearts. The only catch? The Cutters have to decide what is more important, their daughter's life or her soul.

Available on amazon!

About the Author

Jacy Morris is a Native American author who has brought to life zombies, cults, demons, killer boy bands, and spirits. You can learn more about him at the following:

Website: http://jacymorris.com

Email: jacy@jacymorris.com

Facebook:
https://www.facebook.com/JacyMorrisAuthor/

Twitter: https://twitter.com/Vocabulariast

Be sure to check out

THE

DROP

By Jacy Morris

Here is a sneak preview:

PROLOGUE

An excerpt from an article entitled "Whoa-Town Becoming Whoa-World in Record Time" by Anton Russo as Published in *Rolling Stone*

Part of me wants to hate them. Boy bands aren't supposed to be this good. A man, a grown-ass, thirty-year-old man, shouldn't find himself moved by the vocal-stylings of five boys, some not even old enough to drink yet. But here I am, at Wembley Stadium, packed in like cattle in a slaughterhouse chute, ready to stick my head into the kill box and have a hole punched in my cranium.

There is no opening band for Whoa-Town. What sucker would take that gig? Who would want to have the memory of their performance obliterated by the next act, a band that many claim is bigger than the Beatles and the Stones combined? Lofty words. All of us scoffing, bearded, music snobs sneer, knowing full well in our hearts that there is no way anyone means it when they throw out those comparisons. It's just the thing that clichéd, hack journalists say when they can't think of any way of telling people how big a band is or is going to be.

Here I am, standing amid the heat and the hot breath of 90,000 people, the lucky ones who snagged their tickets in that first two minutes before the entire system crashed. Leading to a day in London collectively known as Cry Day, the day that every teenage girl, and many other men, women, and boys christened their cell phones with tears at news that the Whoa-Town show was already sold out.

You'd expect the air to reek of cheap designer-knockoff perfume, hair product and bubblegum. But it doesn't. It smells of something else. It reeks instead of lust and anticipation. The crowd hums with energy; their faces drip sweat even though the stadium's roof is open to the elements. The cool night air can't compete with their fever. Their bodies vibrate, conducting heat at a level that confirms in my mind that spontaneous combustion might actually be a thing. At any moment, the girl next to me, screaming ear-piercing "woos" every thirty seconds or so, might burst into flames.

Before long, we can't take it anymore. Wait... they can't take it. I'm certainly not into any boy band. I'm just here for the story. They begin to chant. When the mother next to me, clad in baggy jeans that go up past her bellybutton, elbows me as encouragement, I make a show of reluctantly joining in. I clap. I yell, "Whoa-Town!" right along with everyone else.

Only when the building quakes from all the stomping, yelling, and clapping does something happen. Just as I am assured that Wembley Stadium will collapse around us before the band ever takes stage, the lights come on, blinding us. The lights fade, dropping faster than my own aloof persona, plunging us into a darkness punctuated by the unwelcome glow of emergency lighting. Around the stadium, tiny rectangular blooms of blue-light illuminate in response. 90,000 people recording when they aren't supposed to be. It is as if the stadium is filled with thousands of mutant fireflies, swaying from side to side as the chant of "Whoa-Town!" thunders through the stadium once again... and then the beat drops.

With a "whoomp," several sparking shapes arc into the air, erupting into gold and crimson starbursts, and screams echo so loudly that I'm not even sure when the screaming stops and the music begins. They're here. Whoa-Town, the boys that will change music and the world forever and I, Anton Russo, was there.

Tragic. Just tragic. - Sebastian

You think that's tragic, check out those *Teen Beat* articles I found. - Katherine

Chapter 1: Walking the Streets

I see this story as more than a job, more than just a fact-finding mission to once again help us cope with the tragedy, with a loss that, in a very real sense, is unprecedented. Many people have tried that. So many. No, if that's all this was, then I would be off somewhere else, looking into a murder or trying to uncover the next dastardly person exploiting the American Relief Organization.

I see this story as a time capsule, a way to help the people of the future. If there's one thing that I learned from my 8th-grade social studies teacher, it's that history is a cycle, and that all things, good or bad, will come around again, hence the term revolution, a circuit, a never-ending loop that only the educated can see. Thinking about what the world has just gone through, and is still going through, I can only shudder at the thought that hundreds of years down the line this will all happen again. So my hope is to write this story, bury it in the ground, and when it's needed, the people of the future can come and dig it up.

People will need to know, not so much the people that are still alive, but the people of the future. The people still alive already know about The Drop. They're so tired of thinking about it that they don't actually want to know the truth of the situation. They can't help but see The Drop around them. Examining it further is just poking at a poorly stitched together wound with a razorblade. Sooner or later it's going to open up. Sooner or later, it's going to bleed. They don't want to know how the knife that stabbed them in the chest was forged. They don't want to know where the steel came from, how the ivory handle was carved from the tusk of a poached elephant. None of that will help them.

But for the people of the future, that's a different story altogether. The Drop was our Black Plague, and just as our knowledge of the spread of the plague prevents it from happening again, this article is vital to preventing another Drop.

I'm in the Big Apple. They call it the Big Rotten Core now. As I walk down Broadway, I'm struck by its similarity to the post-apocalyptic movies I over-consumed as a teenager. The emptiness of the streets, very *I Am Legend.* The newspaper tumbling through the intersection, unchecked like a tumbleweed through a western town, very *The Road.* The sad motherfucker leaning up against the wall, smoking a cigarette, and staring at the cracked and crumbling concrete, very *Book of Eli.*

The street ends at Times Square, once a mega-hub of awesomeness where cowboys played guitar in their underwear and an unceasing cavalcade of electric, sex-themed ads assaulted wayward tourists. It was now just a scene from *The Postman.* There weren't enough people to provide upkeep for the cities. Those that stayed did so because they had become ghosts themselves, haunted by the losses of The Drop. They stuck around, though no more food was coming, except for that which they grew themselves. Though the children didn't play hopscotch on the streets and the stoplights had been turned off, the ghosts remained, remembering the glory of New York and its eight-and-a-half-million residents.

Glass crunches under my boots as I turn and look inside the Disney Store... all those toys just sitting there, no one left to play with them. I step inside. The cash register was busted open a long time ago, but the toys sit waiting. And I can't help but wonder who will actually benefit from the story that I am going to tell.

The next generation, I suppose, the ones that will grow up without music. The ones that will grow up without the internet, they'll want these dolls. They'll want something to play with.

I exit the Disney Store, sick of looking at clownish, Dory plush dolls. I am in time for the show. The man at the end of the street puts a gun in his mouth and pulls the trigger. Blood sprays the wall behind him. I scream like a maniac, but somehow, no one in Times Square hears me... because I'm the only person left alive in a place that was once called "The Crossroads of the World." And I wonder, was that man just waiting for someone to stumble along? Was he waiting for an audience before he killed himself? Or were his sixty days up?

I shudder and call the police. "Hello?... Yeah, there's been a suicide in Times Square... What do you mean three hours?"

I hang up. I go back inside the Disney store, and I grab myself a Dory plushy, and I hold onto it for dear life as the man's blood and brains run down the wall. This was probably the worst vacation idea I had ever had.

Available on amazon now!

Be sure to check out

The Abbey

By Jacy Morris

Here is a sneak preview:

THE ABBEY

PROLOGUE

He would make him scream. So far they had all screamed, their unused voices quaking and cracking with pain that was made even worse by the fact that they were breaking their vows to their Lord, their sole reason for existence. Shattering their vows was their last act on earth, and then they were gone. Now there was only one left. A lone monk had taken flight into the abbey's lower regions, a labyrinthine winding of corridors and catacombs lined with the boxed up remains of the dead and their trinkets.

Brenley Denman's boots clanked off of the rough-hewn, blue stone as he trounced through the abbey's crypts, following the whiff of smoke from the monk's torch and the echo of his harried footsteps. His men were spread out through the underworks, funneling the monk ahead of them, driving him the way hounds drove a fox. The monk would lead them to his den, and then the prize would be theirs. And then the world.

He held his torch up high, watching the flames glimmer off of golden urns and silver swords, ancient relics of a nobility that had long since gone extinct, their glory only known by faded etchings in marble sarcophagi, the remaining glint of their once-prized possessions, and the spiders who built their webs in the darkness. Once they were done with the monk, they would take anything that glittered, but first they needed the talisman, the fabled bauble that resided at the bottom of the mountain the abbey was built on.

Throughout the land, legends of the talisman had been told for decades around hearthfires and inns throughout the isles. Then the tellers had begun to vanish, until the talisman of Inchorgrath and its stories had all but been forgotten. But Denman knew. He remembered the stories his father had told him while they sat around the fire of their stone house, built less than ten yards from the cemetery. His father's knuckles were cracked and dried from hours in the elements digging graves and rifling pockets when no one was looking. He knew secrets when he saw them. His father had first heard the story from the old Celts, the remains of the land's indigenous population, reduced to poverty and begging in the streets. His father said the old Celts' stories were two-thirds bullshit and one-third truth. They told of a relic, a key to the Celts' uprising and reclamation of the land, buried in the deepest part of the tallest mountain on the Isles. Of course, they spoke of regeneration and the return of Gods among men as well, but the relic... that was the important part. That was the part that was worth money. And now, he was here, with his men, ready to make his fortune.

He heard shouts, but it was impossible to tell where they were coming from. Sound echoed and bounced off of the blue, quartzite stone blocks, warping reality. He chose the corridor to his right, quickening his pace, his long legs eating up the distance. His men knew not to start without him, but you never knew when a monk would lash out, going against their discipline and training and earning a sword through the throat for their duplicity. That would be unacceptable to Denman. The monk must scream before he died.

His breathing quickened along with his pace, and he could feel the warmth of anticipation spread through his limbs as his breath puffed into the cold crypt air. Miles... they had come miles through these crypts, twisting and turning, burrowing into the secret heart of the earth, chasing the last monk who skittered through the hallways like a spider. The other monks had all known the secret of the abbey, the power it harbored, the relic it hid in its bowels. To a man, they had sat on their knees, their robes collecting condensation in the green grass of the morning, refusing to divulge the abbey's mysteries.

They had died, twisted, mangled and beaten. But still, all he could pull from them were the screams, musical expulsions of the throat that he ended with a smile as he dragged the razor-fine edge of his knife across their throats. Their blood had bubbled out, vivid against the morning sun, to splash on the grass.

When there was only one left, they had let him go. The youngest monk in the abbey, grown to manhood, but still soft about the face, his intelligent eyes filled with horror, stood and ran, his robe stained with the pooled blood of the monks that had died to his left and right. He was like one of the homing pigeons they used in the lowlands, leading them to home... to the relic. They had chased him, hooting and hollering the whole way, their voices and taunts driving the monk before them like a fox. The chase would end at his burrow; it always did.

Ahead, he heard laughing, and with that Denman knew that the chase was at an end. He rounded one last corner to see the monk being worked over by his men, savage pieces of stupidity who were good for two things, lifting heavy objects and killing people. Denman waved his hand and they let the suffering monk go. The monk sagged to the ground, his head bent over, his eyes leaking tears. He sobbed in silence.

Denman stood in the secret of the crypt, a room at the heart of the mountain, the place where legends hid. How deep had they gone? At first there had been stairs, but then they had reached a deeper part of the crypt where the corridors twisted and turned, the floor pitched ever downward. Time and distance had lost all meaning in the breast of the world. How long had it taken them to carve this place, the monks working in silence to protect their treasure? Hundreds of years? A thousand?

The room was simple and small, as the order's aesthetics demanded, filled by Denman and the nine men that he had brought to take the abbey's secrets. Wait, one was missing. He looked at his men, brutal pieces of humanity, covered in dirt, mud and blood. The boy wasn't there. Denman shrugged. He would find his way down eventually.

The walls of the room were blue-gray, stone blocks stacked one on top of the other without the benefit of mortar, the weight of the mountain providing the only glue that was needed. The only other features of the room were an alcove with two thick, tallow candles in cheap tin holders and an ancient oak table.

The smoke from his men's torches hung in the air, creating a stinging miasma that stung his eyes. Brenley Denman squatted next to the monk and used his weathered hand to raise the monk's head by his chin. He looked into the monk's eyes, and instead of the fear that he expected to see, there was something else.

"What is this? Defiance?" he asked, amused by the monk's bravado. Denman stood and kicked the monk in the mouth with his boot, a shit-covered piece of leather that was harder than his heart; teeth and blood decorated the stones.

"Where is it?" he asked the monk. There was no answer. Denman had expected none. Say what you will about the Lord's terrestrial servants, but they were loyal... which made everything more difficult... more exhilarating. Denman was a man that loved a challenge.

He handed his torch to one of his men, a broken-faced simpleton whose only gifts were strength and the ability to do what he was told. Denman knew that he would need both hands to make the monk sing his secrets.

"Hand me the Tearmaker," he said to another of his men. Radan, built like a rat with stubby arms and powerful legs, reached to his belt and produced a knife, skinny and flexible, designed not so much for murder as it was for removing savory meat from skin and fat. It made excellent work of fish, and it would most likely prove delightfully deft at making a tight-lipped monk break his vows.

As he reached out to take the proffered knife from his man, the monk scrambled to his feet and dove for the alcove. Before they could stop him, the monk grasped both of the candle sticks and yanked on them. The candlesticks rose into the air. Rusted, metal chains were affixed to their bases, and they clanked against the surrounding stone of the alcove as the monk pulled on them.

The distant sound of stones grinding upon stones reverberated throughout the crypt. Somewhere, something was moving. Denman glared at the monk. The robed figure dropped the candlesticks and turned to face them. With his head cast downward, he reached into the folds of his robe and produced a rosary. He folded his hands and began to pray, beads moving through his fingers, his lips moving without making sound.

The crypt shook as an unseen weight clattered through the halls of the crypt. Dust fell from the ceiling, hanging in the air, buoyed upwards by the tumbling smoke of their torches.

"What have you done?" Denman asked.

The monk did not respond. Instead, he reached into the hanging sleeve of one of his robes and produced a small stone thimble, roughly-made and ancient. It was shiny and black, the type of black that seemed to steal the light from the room. The monk put it up to his mouth, hesitated for a second and then swallowed it, grimacing in pain as the object slid down his throat.

In the hallway behind them, the grinding had stopped. The crypt was silent, but for the guttering of the torches and their own breathing. "Go see what happened," he said to the oaf and the rat. The other men followed them, leaving Denman alone with the monk and his unceasing, silent supplications to the Lord above.

Denman forced the monk onto the oak table. He offered little resistance. With Tearmaker in his hand, Denman began to carve the skin lovingly off of the monk's fingers. First, he carved a circle around the man's fingers, then a line. With the edge of his knife, he prodded a corner of the skin up, and then, grasping tightly, he ripped the skin away from the muscle and bone, dropping the wet flesh onto the ground. He did this to each finger, one by one. Sweat stood out on Denman's brow, and the monk had yet to scream. He hadn't so much as gasped or hissed in pain. He was turning out to be more work than he was worth.

Except for the blood pulsing from his skinned fingers, he appeared to be asleep, his eyes softly closed.

"Where is it, you bastard?" There was no response but for the bleeding.

Denman pulled the monk's robe up around his waist. It was a quick jump, but he was eager to be done with the man on the table. Usually, he would take his time with a challenge like the monk, savoring the sensation of skin ripping from muscle and bone, but he could feel the weight of the mountain about him, its walls shrinking with every minute. Sweat covered his body, and the monk's calm demeanor was unnerving.

Radan rounded the corner at a run, his body dripping with sweat and panic on his face. He skidded to a stop, his boots grinding dust into the blue stones. "We're sealed in here," he said.

Denman looked at the monk lying on the table. His hand gripped Tearmaker tight. "What have you done?" The monk lay there, his eyes closed, a look of peace on his face. "What have you done!" he screamed, jabbing the knife into the monk's ribs. Then Denman saw the monk's hands. Where before his index and pointer finger had been reduced to skinless chunks of muscle and bone dripping blood on the table, there was now skin. "Impossible," Denman whispered.

The monk's eyes snapped open, and finally, Denman got the scream that he had been waiting for.

Available on amazon now!

Be sure to check out

THE PIED

PIPER

OF HAMELIN

By Jacy Morris

Here is a sneak preview:

The Pied Piper of Hamelin

Prologue: The River Weser

The boat captain sailed down the river, the wind ruffling his long, salt-and-pepper locks. It was a fine day. His ship was laden with goods, and he was relishing the prospect of turning a nice profit for himself and his crew. He should have been happy, ecstatic, singing shanties that would turn a barmaid's face red, but he wasn't.

The captain sniffed inward, pulling a grimy film of mucus into the back of his throat. He hacked up a thick glob and deposited it into the Weser River. He could taste the blood in it. His men were no better. Though they were ill, they still did their jobs. After all, a boatswain who couldn't earn his keep wouldn't receive his full share. On top of that, as an example to his men, the captain continued to work, stalking the decks and shouting out orders, though all he wanted to do was go down below and curl up in his cabin. He felt as if his head was trying to split in half, and he had an uncomfortable swelling in his groin that sent sharp pains through his entire body every time he moved.

Out of the corner of his eye, he spied furtive movement. Goddamn rats, he thought to himself. He would have to see if he could find some sort of boat cat in the next town. He consulted his charts, hand-drawn, passed down from captain to captain, and saw that the next village would be Hamelin.

It was an uppity berg; the mayor was trying to turn it into Rome from what the goodfolk at the pier told him.

They had no need of Rome in this part of the world. What they needed was good strong ale, women with weak morals, and more good strong ale. Or maybe that's just what he needed.

A chilly breeze washed over the river, and the captain pulled his jacket tighter, gritting his teeth at the sharp pain the movement caused him. Underneath his arms, there were more swellings, unnatural lumps that seemed as if they were nothing but bundles of nerves. Pulling the jacket tighter had been like jabbing a flame-heated knife, point first, into each of his armpits.

Without warning, he began to cough like he had never coughed before. Black spots swam in front of his eyes, and for a brief moment, he thought, This is it. This is how I die. But then the coughing passed, and he was able to grab a raspy breath of air. The muscles in his back felt worse for wear, and he spat a wad of red-flecked phlegm into the river.

The breeze kicked up again, but this time, he didn't bother to readjust his jacket. Instead, he let the wind wash over him, evaporating the fever sweat from his brow.

"Captain," his first mate said, "Old Gert is dead."

It took a while for the words to sink into his fever-addled mind, but when they did, he did the only thing he could do. "Pitch him over the side, lad. It's a water-burial for him."

Normally, they would keep the body in the cold hull of the ship so that his family could bury him proper, but with all of the rats on board, it would be more dignified to give him to the river than to let those furry bastards make a meal out of him.

The first mate scuttled off to do his bidding without question. That was good. It meant that the crew didn't think he was responsible for the plague that had descended upon them. Sailors were a superstitious lot, but the captain had never held stock with the ridiculous notions of superstition. But that didn't mean that his crew wouldn't turn on him if more started to die.

He heard the sound of scurrying across the deck. "What the hell was that?" he wondered aloud. Spinning around quickly, he caught sight of movement out of the corner of his eye. It was another rat, a huge one. He chased it across the deck for a few steps, but then stopped due to the pain. After the first couple of steps, the lumps in his groin shot fire through his entire body. He vowed to find a cat when they got to Hamelin. In the meantime, he said a prayer for Old Gert as his body splashed into the river.

The rats watched and listened, the fleas on their backs oblivious to everything but the flesh in front of them and the blood underneath.

Available on amazon now!

Printed in Great Britain
by Amazon

46472171R00119